D0909076

Dustin Grubbs

ONE★MAN SHOW

Dustin Grubbs
ONE★MAN SHOW

John J. Bonk

LITTLE, BROWN AND COMPANY

New York ᧬ Boston

Little, Brown and Company

Time Warner Book Group
1271 Avenue of the Americas, New York, NY 10020
Visit our Web site at www.lb-kids.com

First Edition: September 2005

Library of Congress Cataloging-in-Publication Data
Bonk, John J.
 Dustin Grubbs : one-man show / John J. Bonk – 1st ed.
  p. cm.
 Summary: A sixth-grader, who longs to see his name in lights, recounts life at
Buttermilk Falls Elementary in preparation for the school drama production.
 ISBN 0-316-15636-1
 [1. Schools – Fiction. 2. Actors and actresses – Fiction. 3. Theater – Fiction.
4. Humorous stories.] I. Title.

PZ7.B6416Du   2005
[Fic] – dc22   2004021268

Cover photography by Roger Hagadone
Jacket design by Tracy Shaw
The text was set in Regent, and the display type is Hornpype ITC.

10 9 8 7 6 5 4 3 2 1

Q-FF

Printed in the United States of America

For all the friends, family, teachers, and classmates
who've made me smile, laugh, gasp, or holler,
and have (in some way or another)
wriggled their way into the pages of this book

Dustin Grubbs

ONE★MAN SHOW

Prologue

(As Heard on Televisions across the Nation)

You'll crack a rib laughing at today's encore episode of *Double Take*, starring Jeremy Jason Wilder! Stay tuned for America's zaniest, *insaniest* sitcom twins, Buddy and Bailey Bickford, as they butt their way into Laugh-Fest Saturday Morning!

Double Take is brought to you by Keggler's Crustacean Crunch cereal — fortified with the forty-five essential vitamins and minerals found in seafood. Dive into a bowlful today! But no channel surfing, kids, 'cause we're coming right back.

Chapter 1

If You Can See Them, They Can See You

"TODAY, SIXTH GRADE – TOMORROW, THE UNIVERSE!"
was splashed across the hall bulletin board outside our classroom. Below it were index cards saying what we wanted to be when we grew up. If things worked out as planned, Room 2C would crank out two doctors, one dentist, three teachers, a pet hypnotist (don't ask), five baseball players, three football players, four basketball players, two stay-at-home moms, and one actor. Guess who?

Dustin Grubbs. Age 11. Actor.
I hope to change the world through my meaningful performances in movies, on television, and on the Broadway stage.

My dad used to be a stand-up comic. Probably still is, for all I know. So I guess show-biz is in my blood. Still, putting *actor* on that card took guts. It was like writing *wizard* or *superhero* – something impossible to become. And it looked totally lame next to:

Elizabeth T. Snodd. Age 10½. Neurosurgeon.
I hope to change the world by contributing to advancements in brain research and saving lives.

With that in mind, a good place to start my story is backstage at Buttermilk Falls Elementary, where I was getting ready to make my theatrical debut in about –

"Fifteen minutes to showtime, people!"

– in about fifteen minutes. That was our principal, Mr. Futterman, disappearing through the red velvet curtain with a "what the heck are we in for?" look on his face. Futterman used to be a gym teacher, once upon a time. He'd traded in his whistle and sneakers for a suit and tie, but inside he was still a big jock. To him, putting on *The Castle of the Crooked Crowns* was nothing but a royal pain. To me it was everything.

"Betty Batter bought some butter . . ." I was channeling my nervous energy into a killer tongue twister, worrying myself sick about my best friend, Wally, who'd never made it back from lunch. "But, said she, this butter's bitter. . . ." I had the starring role of Jingle Jangles the Jester. Wally "the Walrus"

Dorkin was playing the King. "If I put it in my batter, it will make my batter bitter." You're gonna like Wally – everyone does. When he doesn't screw things up, that is.

Backstage looked like a loony bin. Our teacher/goddess, Miss Honeywell, was busy gluing mustaches on the girls who were playing men. The rest of the girls were testing out the twirl factor of their long medieval dresses – all except for my leading lady, Pepper. She was on her knees, with three-inch nails sticking out of her mouth, hammering the castle wall. Pepper Pew had a lot more grit in her than most girls. With a name like that slapped on her from birth, I guess she didn't have much of a choice.

"Hey, Pep, have you seen Wally?" I asked.

She shrugged.

"For cryin' out loud, where's the Walrus?"

"Shhh, Miss Honeywell'll hear," Pepper said. "You don't want to get him in trouble, do ya?"

"Well, she's gonna find out eventually. We can't do the play without the King!"

"Oh, right," she said, looking up at me, brushing her red bangs out of her eyes. "Shouldn't you get changed?"

"I can't. Wally's bringing my costume."

"Oh," Pepper said, giving the scenery another whack.

"You should wrap that up," I told her. "The audience is coming in."

"You got it, chief."

I ran to Felix Plunket, who was tugging on his tights and rehearsing his Prince lines to a potted plant. I swear his face was nearly as green as the ficus. Felix was the fidgety type, but he was the only other boy who'd agreed to do the play besides Wally and me. (And only after I bribed him with a brand-new NBA all-surface basketball.) He hadn't seen Wally either.

I was about to start banging my head on a piece of scenery when Wally rushed in, all blotchy faced. He was lugging a load of costumes over his shoulder and carrying his bassoon case. Oh, in case you don't know, a bassoon is a woodwind instrument that looks like an old stovepipe and sounds like a strangled duck. Wally's head turned purple and inflated to three times its normal size when he blew into it. That can't be healthy.

"Finally!" I said.

"Sorry, Dust –," Wally said, gasping for air like a drowning man. "Ran home for lunch . . . to pick up the costumes. My ma was just finishing the last one. . . . I was halfway back to school when I realized . . . I forgot my bassoon!"

"So?"

"I have a lesson right after school."

"How many costumes do you need, anyway? The King is only in, like, three scenes."

Mrs. Dorkin must've cleaned out Sew What?, the local fabric store. Wally wasn't exactly petite. Then again, I was a stick. Together we formed the number 10.

"They're not *all* mine," Wally said, holding out the pile of costumes. "The striped one on top is yours. Take it."

I grabbed the first hanger and ripped through the clear plastic that was covering my costume.

"I took that shortcut through the park and made it back in, like, twelve minutes – carrying all this stuff," Wally said, checking his watch. "That's got to be a personal best."

"Uh-huh. Oh, that reminds me." I turned to the rest of the cast. "Take off your watches, everybody," I announced. "They didn't exist in the Middle Ages."

Believe it or not, Buttermilk Falls Elementary hadn't put on a play since around the Middle Ages. Okay, the mideighties. We had a basketball team, cheerleaders, our own mini-Olympics – but no plays. What started out as a class project was about to be performed for the whole school, thanks to Miss Honeywell. She said the play was just too good not to share with the world. I owed her big time. Not only did she cast me in the lead, she made me her AD. That's short for *assistant director.*

In a secluded spot behind the back curtain, I wriggled into what were probably a pair of Mrs. Dorkin's yellow panty hose and a stained pillowcase with armholes. I'd made my own jester's shoes out of my aunt Birdie's pointy house slippers, and braided three of my dad's old ties into a nifty belt. I'd found them in the attic, in a box marked *Destroy!* They were left over from when he used to work at Apex Plastics – usually referred to by my father as "the job that's slowly sucking the life out of me."

"Dustin, how darling you look!" Miss Honeywell said in her Southern twang when I stepped out from the shadows.

"Darling" wasn't exactly the look I was going for.

"I really should check on our class," she said, standing at the prop table, looking frazzled. "They're just sitting out there unattended. Do you think you could finish this prop check for me?"

"Sure thing."

She handed me a clipboard, and I held it up against myself (where – if I were a statue – a fig leaf would be). Nothing was showing, but I still felt exposed.

"Oh, and be a sweetheart and make sure Leonard has his cues?"

One "sweetheart" from her and my legs got all noodley. She was prettier than any teacher should be, but she still had a lot of "spit and vinegar" in her, as Granny Grubbs would say.

"One rubber chicken – check. Six juggling balls – check. One paper scroll –"

Darlene Deluca, who was doing leaps across the stage, did one leap too many and rammed into me. My clipboard went flying.

"*Oww!*"

"Sorry," she said, handing the clipboard back to me. She leaned in close with her eyes shut, and I thought she was going to give me a good-luck kiss. You never knew with Darlene.

"Do I need more Passion Plum?" she asked.

"What?"

"Eye shadow!"

"I don't think so," I said. She had enough goop on her face for ten Halloweens. "But Pepper could use a little help with her makeup. One plastic rose – check."

Darlene gave me a look like I'd asked her to clean up after queasy elephants.

"I still don't know why Pepper Pee-U is the Princess," she said. "She should've been the Minstrel, instead of Cynthia. She's practically a boy anyway."

"Not this again," I said.

"She's supposed to be royalty, and she's wearing a bedsheet!"

"Well, at least it's queen-size."

"Puh-lease. Check out my gown. It's the haute couture bridesmaid's dress I wore to my cousin Trish's wedding," Darlene said, doing a runway-model pose. "Definitely something a princess would wear."

"Yeah, but it's all wrong for your character," I said. "Lady Pickerel is supposed to be, like, sixty. Maybe you and Pepper should switch costumes."

"No way, José," Darlene snarled. "I ain't getting her cooties on it."

"Okay, just help her with her makeup, then. She really needs your expert advice. One jester's stick – check."

"Well, I do have an extra pair of false eyelashes. They might draw attention away from her unibrow."

One con job – check!

I headed toward Leonard Shempski, the techie, to go over his cues. That's when I noticed a small peephole in the right side of the curtain. I stuck my face up to it and closed one eye. I could see the whole audience.

The first-graders were in the front row, jumpy as grasshoppers on a grill. Futterman was blabbing at Miss Honeywell, next to my class, somewhere in the middle seats. The eighth-graders were filing in at the back, looking too cool for school.

"Hey, it's a full house!" I said, grabbing Wally, who was lost in the lime green getup he was pulling over his head.

"Well, it's a school assembly – they *had* to come," he said. "It's not like they *paid* for tickets or anything."

Wally could suck the joy out of a birthday party on the beach.

"Let me see." He shoved me aside and looked through the hole. "Oh, man. It's packed."

"I told you. SRO – standing room only. Isn't that great?"

"I guess," he said.

"Look, a lunchroom lady just snuck in the back door."

"Dust? I swear, I can't remember my first line in scene three."

"Don't do this to me, Wally."

The look on his face told me he wasn't kidding. It was a good thing a script was attached to the clipboard. I flipped to scene three.

"'Why do you look so forlorn, Daughter?'"

"'Why do you look so forlorn?'" Wally repeated. "Why did they have to put words like *forlorn* in it? Nobody knows what that means, anyway."

"It means sad," I said. "That's how they used to talk back then."

"And am I supposed to say my line and *then* cross to center, or say my line *while* I'm crossing?"

Wally was clearly losing his mind.

"It doesn't really matter, Wal." I gave him a pat on the back, 'cause it looked as if he needed it. "But say your line and *then* cross."

"Line, then cross."

"Ten minutes, people! Ten minutes!" Futterman flew by in a blur.

"I have to go to the bathroom," Wally said, bouncing. "It's an emergency."

"Just work fast."

Wally disappeared, and I had the hole to myself again. Darlene tried to wedge her fat head in front of mine, but I wouldn't let her, so she ended up peeking under the curtain.

"Remember, if you can see them, they can see you!"

I knew Miss Honeywell was back before she even said a word. Her peach-pie perfume was a dead giveaway.

"Can y'all gather round?" Miss Honeywell said. She'd transferred to our school in September, from the South, so she said "y'all" a lot. The cast mobbed her.

"Ooh, I'm all goose-pimply," she said. "You kids ought to be percolating with pride from all the hard work you've done – especially our star, Dustin Grubbs!"

I already felt like the luckiest kid on the planet, and now Miss Honeywell was gushing over me, smiling so wide her eyeballs disappeared. Life was good.

"I'm not supposed to say anything, 'cause nothing's confirmed yet," Miss Honeywell said in a hushed voice, "but I've just heard some thrilling news, y'all. Someone *very* special is going to be in our –"

Futterman zipped by, and Miss Honeywell stopped short.

"What is it, Miss Honeywell?" a bunch of us said. "Tell us."

"No, I'd better not. I've said too much already." She mimed locking her lips with a key and tossing it over her shoulder. "But if the rumor is true, Dustin and Wallace will be as tickled as two june bugs in a feather factory!"

"Is that a good thing?" I asked.

The backstage lights went out, then on again.

"I'd better get back to my seat, lickety-split. Break a leg, kids."

"Break a leg, Miss Honeywell!" everyone shouted. Which was stupid. It's like saying "happy birthday" back to someone wishing you a happy birthday.

"What did I miss?" Wally said, rushing back. He was all over me like sticky on tape. "What rumor? I heard the word *rumor*."

"Good question."

"Five minutes!" Futterman's voice boomed out of nowhere.

"Oh, no. I have to go to the bathroom again!" Wally said, racing away.

I grabbed my jester's hat from the prop table and ran to the curtain hole to get one last look. *Was someone special out in the audience? Was it a talent scout? A Broadway director?* I scanned the seats for anyone unusual. The houselights dimmed.

"Are you kids ready to go?" Futterman said, poking his head around the curtain. "After 'The Star-Spangled Banner' I'm going to give a quick intro, and then you're up."

Backstage went black. My toes curled inside my curly-toed shoes, and the last of my saliva dried up. *Deep breaths,* I told myself.

The audience was screeching, "And the rocket's red glaaare," I was back to "Betty Batter bought some buttering," and that's when it started.

Clang-clang! Clang-clang!

It was so bust-an-eardrum loud that the scenery vibrated. I was hoping a really noisy ice-cream truck was passing by.

Clang-clang!

But I knew differently.

Chapter 2

Drills, Chills, and Spills

I was forlorn.

I used to love fire drills. I always thought of them as bonus minirecesses. But sometimes you can take two great things, slap them together, and end up with a disaster on your hands – like all-you-can-eat sundaes and the Gut Buster roller coaster at Venture Quest Park.

Or plays and fire drills.

The cast got swallowed up by the crowd jamming through the exit doors of the auditorium. It's a good thing it was freakishly warm for March, 'cause I didn't have my jacket – or my pants. The school yard was a total mishmash. No neat fire-drill rows. Pepper and I were smooshed between the second-grade class and some rowdy seventh-graders. Our class was nowhere in sight.

Out in bright daylight I was suddenly aware of the red

circles I had painted on my cheeks. Not to mention the curly-toed shoes, droopy tights, and pillowcase tunic. Breezes were blowing where no breeze had gone before.

"Hey, Dust Bin, nice dress!" Travis Buttrick said. "You got a purse to match?"

"Yeah, I borrowed it from your mother," I said, which didn't make sense. But people don't like it when you mention their mothers.

Travis was a year older than me, and he was already sprouting facial hair. You know the type. Rich. Spoiled. Kicked out of every private school in the Midwest.

"Oh, yeah? Well, *your* mother just called – she wants her lipstick back," he said. (See, I told you about the "mother" thing.)

"Oh, stick a sock in it, Buttrick," Pepper said.

"What's the matter, Dust Bin?" Travis said. "You make your girlfriend do all your fighting for you?"

"Just ignore him, Pepper," I said, yanking her away.

The fire drill was taking a lot longer than usual. Teachers were trying to round up their classes, but some kids escaped to the swings and monkey bars. Others were picking on innocent costumed bystanders.

Derek, one of Travis's boneheaded friends, started sniffing the air around Pepper.

"Oh, no, I'm gonna sneeze!" he said. "Ah . . . aaah . . . *ah-chooo!*"

"How original," Pepper said. "Can't you Neanderthals come up with a new one?"

"Now, Pepper," I said, "you mustn't speak ill of the brain-dead."

"Pepper sounds like a dog's name," Travis said. "Sit, Pepper! Stay, Pepper! How did your parents know you'd turn out to be such a dog?"

"Okay, knock it off!" I said, stepping forward.

Travis's arm sprang out at me with his fingers in flicking position, like a bee ready to sting. I tried dodging, and he knocked off my jester's hat.

"Hey!"

"You said 'knock it off,'" he said, laughing.

Miss Honeywell had made me that hat with her own two hands. It was constructed out of multicolored felt and had five floppy points with pom-poms on the tips. When I bent over to pick up the hat, Travis kicked it out from under me. Then he grabbed it and threw it to Derek. The next thing I knew, they were playing keep-away.

"Give it back!" I shouted.

"Look at me, I'm king of the dweebs!" Travis had my hat on and was dancing around like a drunken marionette.

Why is there never a teacher around when you need one?

People other than Travis Buttrick suck-ups were starting to watch. We had to get even. Pepper came up with a plan and whispered it into my ear. I gave her a "let's go for it" nod, and we assumed our positions.

"Okay," Pepper said, "on the count of three . . ."

"*One*." We turned our backs to the enemy.

"*Two*." We yelled, "Hey, Buttrick! Wanna see a butt trick?"

"*Three*." We bent over, lifted our costumes, and shook our rear ends.

It was excellent. Even Travis's friends were howling. It wasn't exactly the performance I thought I'd be giving that day, but as my aunt Olive says, "If life hands you lemons, make lemonade."

Pepper and I were shaking our bottoms and stirring our lemonade when I saw a pair of deformed high heels stomping toward us. A whiff of stale perfume slapped me in the face. I was getting to be an expert at recognizing teachers by their smells. While Miss Honeywell's was a perfect combination of peach pie and vanilla, this stink bomb was a way-too-flowery blast from the past.

"Mr. Grubbs! Miss Pew!"

It was Mrs. Eugenia Sternhagen, my old second-grade teacher. Ah, yes, I remember it well: an overpowering blend of Country Garden toilet bowl cleaner and Dr. Desmond's wart remover.

"Save your shenanigans for the stage!" she shrieked.

Pepper and I shot upright. Birds stopped chirping. The American flag stopped rustling.

"Sorry, Mrs. Sternhagen." Those words seemed so familiar to my lips.

"This is a serious situation we have here," she said.

Is she talking about the fire drill or the butt trick?

Mrs. Sternhagen was lugging around one of her trademark shopping bags. You never knew what she was going to pull out of those things – a stapler? comfortable shoes? her pet tarantula? Sometimes she'd recruit a few of her second-graders to carry the bags for her. I remember – I used to be one of them. Slave labor.

"This isn't just a drill," she said, digging around in her bag. She pulled out a tissue and handed it to me; I guess I must've been leaking. I blew my nose and handed it back. "Principal Futterman informed me that there was a small grease fire in the cafeteria. So, best behavior!"

Her favorite saying. It made me want to shove pencils in my ears. Or hers.

"Did they put the fire out?" Pepper asked. "Is everyone all right?"

"Everything is under control," Mrs. Sternhagen said. "It's a shame about your play, children. I understand you worked very hard."

Wow, kind words. That was unusual from someone with a personality you could store meat in.

"The whole thing was this guy's idea," Pepper said, punching me on the shoulder.

"Mine and Miss Honeywell's," I said. "We're still doing the play today, right?"

"It's doubtful," Mrs. Sternhagen said. "Perhaps Principal Futterman will reschedule it."

"Perhaps"? What does she mean "perhaps"?

"I seem to recall you had the acting bug back when you were in my class," she said to me. "You were so enthusiastic about our little Christmas pageant."

"Uh-huh."

She'd given me one measly line. Still, it was my first taste of applause. I was hooked.

"Mr. Donovan! Miss Oliver! Best behavior!" Mrs. Sternhagen barked, snapping her fingers at her second-graders. One of them had probably scratched an itch or adjusted a bow or something. "There's always a mischief maker in the bunch."

"This drill is taking forever," Pepper mumbled.

"Patience is a virtue," Mrs. Sternhagen said. "So, Mr. Grubbs, speaking of mischief makers, how is your big brother? Gordon, was it?"

"Fine, I guess. He's at Fenton High."

"Hmm, I'm pleasantly surprised to hear that. I'll never forget what a handful that boy was."

My sixteen-year-old brother, Gordy, had a nickname when he was at Buttermilk Falls Elementary: Trouble. And I had to prove to every new teacher from day one that I wasn't going to be a carbon copy. "Grubbs?" they'd say, tensing up. "Are you Gordon Grubbs's brother?" Lying wasn't really an option, so I'd answer, "Yeah, but only by birth."

Mrs. Sternhagen fished out a small tube of hand cream from her shopping bag. "Well, it's a good thing you didn't follow in his footsteps," she said. "But when I catch you pulling stunts like this on the playground, it makes me wonder."

Okay, you made your point, lady. Let's drop it.

"It all comes down to the family unit." She squeezed a blob of lotion onto her palms and rubbed them together furiously. "And it can't be easy in your circumstances. Am I right, Mr. Grubbs?"

I had an overwhelming urge to kick Eugenia's chubby ankles. Slamming Gordy was one thing, but leave the rest of my family out of it. I had to say something. The words were already forming in my mouth.

"Am I right, Mr. Grubbs?" she repeated, rubbing her hands together like a mad scientist coming up with an evil scheme.

I glanced at Pepper, then locked eyes with Mrs. Sternhagen. My face felt like a red-hot briquette. I got my nerve up, took a deep breath of wart remover, and said, "Yes, ma'am."

The green metal doors sprang open, and Pepper and I got swept away by the mob spilling back into the school. Something rammed me from behind.

"Yeoww!"

I collided with Pepper and we both hit the ground.

"Enjoy your trip?" Travis said, laughing the devil's laugh. "See ya next fall!"

He crumpled my jester's hat and lined it at me, then melted into the crowd. I must've banged my head, 'cause there was definite pain on the left side. No blood, but things were getting whirly.

"You're roadkill, Buttrick!" Pepper shouted. Her sheet-turned-costume was ripped all the way up one side.

The stampede just kept coming. I guess when you're rolling around on the ground in a crazy costume, people think you must be doing it on purpose.

"Hello!" I yelled. "The King's Jester and the beautiful Princess are being trampled to death!"

"Omigod, are you guys all right? What happened?"

I squinted up at two droopy socks. I think they were attached to the little knock-kneed girl who lived next door to me.

"Here!" she said, balling up her sweater and shoving it under my head like a pillow. "Don't move, Dustin Grubbs. I'm going for help!"

The next thing I remember was having a sneezing fit – probably 'cause the sweater was covered in orange cat hair. I scrunched my eyes closed to wait for the pain in my head to pass. But when I opened them again I was lying on a cot, with the nurse's office spinning around me.

Chapter 3

Famous

"What's your name? What's your teacher's name? What grade are you in? What school do you go to?"

Nurse Opal was hovering over me, firing off questions like a criminal investigator.

"Huh? Can you repeat that?"

She went through the same list again, but this time I paid closer attention.

"Dustin Grubbs, Miss Honeywell, sixth, Buttermilk Falls Elementary."

"Excellent," the nurse said, adjusting the ice pack on my forehead. "Now just lie still. You whacked your head but good. How did that happen?"

"I guess I must've tripped."

Ratting on someone was like extra-credit homework – it just wasn't done.

"Well, you're going to be fine, thanks to that little girl Ella something-or-other. You can thank your lucky stars she ran to get me."

"Who?"

"Skinny little thing covered in freckles. Braces make her talk funny."

"Oh. LMNOP."

"What's that now?"

"Ellen Mennopi. Everybody calls her LMNOP. She's this weird little girl who lives next door to me. I rescued her cat from the roof of her garage a few years ago, and she hasn't stopped bugging me since."

"Sounds like someone has a little crush."

"Yeah, my whole body just had a little crush!"

Nurse Opal sprayed something that stung like acid on my scraped elbow, but I didn't scream – too loudly.

"So what's the deal with Pepper?" I asked. "Is she all right?"

"She's back in class. Strong as an ox, that one."

"My head is frostbitten," I said, removing the bag of ice.

"Leave it. It'll help with the swelling."

"I think the swelling's doing just fine on its own."

I put the ice pack back on my lump, which was the size of Pittsburgh, and took a deep breath. The tiny room we were in smelled like the inside of a vitamin bottle.

"Nurse Opal, could you please hurry?" I said. "We still might be doing *The Castle of the Crooked Crowns*."

"Oh, you're not going to be doing any play today, young man," she said, sticking a Band-Aid on my elbow. "You've got yourself quite a nasty bump on your noggin."

"So? Whatever happened to 'The show must go on'? Whatever happened to 'in sickness and in health'? 'Neither snow nor rain, nor gloom of night . . .'"

"I think that's the motto of the U.S. Postal Service – with wedding vows mixed in."

"No play? Great," I said, feeling even more white-hot hatred for Travis Buttrick. "Just great."

Nurse Opal started shining a little flashlight in my eyes. Her face got real close to mine, and all I could see were her wiry, gray nose hairs. She had mega coffee breath.

"Firemen running through the halls," she mumbled. "Mrs. Klumpsky, that nice cafeteria lady, with a second-degree burn. We can go for weeks at a time without so much as a stubbed toe, and then – lordy, when it rains it pours."

She was staring into my eyeballs as if she were trying to see clear through to my brain. Then she switched off the flashlight and sighed.

"Well, you don't seem to have a concussion, thank goodness," she said. "Now just lie back and rest for a while. Your mom'll be here to pick you up soon."

"My mom?" I tried to get up, but she pushed me back down. She was unusually strong for such a doughy lady. "You didn't tell her I was in a play, did you?"

"No. I just said that you had a little accident. Nothing serious."

"Good. I should get dressed. Where're my real clothes?"

"Your little friend went to fetch them," Nurse Opal said. "I won't ask – but it seems to me any mother would be proud as Punch to have their kid starring in the school play."

Yeah, right. It's not easy keeping secrets in a small town, but somehow I managed to hide the whole play thing from Mom. She wasn't a mean mom or anything, just still a little fragile from the divorce. Okay, a lot fragile. Once I heard her tell Gordy, "The day your father stepped onto a stage was the day this family started falling apart." I didn't want to risk her knowing that her only decent son was about to step onto a stage too.

"So, your mom works at Jack Sprat Donuts?" Nurse Opal said, tidying up. "On Clearwater Road?"

"Mm-hm. Just got promoted to assistant manager."

"How wonderful. That place has been around for years. We used to have a nickname for it – now, what did we used to call it?"

"The Donut Hole," I said.

"Bingo!"

"Everyone still calls it that."

Okay, no more small talk. I stared at the door, hoping my clothes would make an appearance before Mom did. Finally LMNOP burst into the room, all hyper and winded.

"Nurse Opal! Here's his stuff!" she lisped. She practically tripped over herself coming toward me. "Omigod, Dustin Grubbs, how're you feeling?"

"Just peachy." I grabbed my street clothes and sneakers from her and dashed behind the changing screen.

"Oh, crud," I said. "My socks aren't here."

"Oops, sorry," I heard LMNOP say.

"That girl is running herself ragged for you," Nurse Opal said. "Not even a thank-you?"

"Thanks."

"Too late. She's gone."

"What rotten luck," I said, fighting into my stiff jeans. "I can't believe this is happening to me."

"Oh, you're going to be just fine," Nurse Opal said. "That lump'll go down in no time."

"Not that, the play. We came so close to doing it, and now –"

"Cheer up, hon. I'm sure it's just being postponed. In the meantime, you must be excited about that famous kid transferring into your class, huh?"

"What? Who?"

Did she really just say that, or were my ears hallucinating?

"Didn't Miss Honeywell tell you?"

"No!" I said, shooting around the changing screen. "What are you talking about?"

"Oh, Jiminy Cricket, maybe I wasn't supposed to let the cat out of the bag."

"Too late. Bag open, cat meowing. What famous kid?"

"Forget I said anything."

"Please! You don't have to actually say the name. I'll ask twenty questions and you can nod yes or no."

"Just keep icing your head off and on," Nurse Opal said, ducking into the outer office. "Your mom'll be here any minute."

I chased after her and saw a white blur disappear into the faculty restroom across the hall.

"Is it a boy or girl?" I called. "Movie-star famous or National Spelling Bee-champion famous?"

I went back into her office and stretched out on the cot. Still a little woozy. No wonder Miss Honeywell was so wigged out before. Someone famous was coming! I closed my eyes and saw the word *FAMOUS* spelled out in flashing light-bulbs. Then I shook my head like an Etch A Sketch to erase it. I didn't have enough info, and I thought my head might explode from the countless possibilities. I forced my mind to wander.

I thought about how "Jack Sprat" was a strange name for a doughnut shop since, according to the poem, "Jack Sprat could eat no fat" and doughnuts are deep fried in oil. I wondered why someone with as bad a lisp as LMNOP's would name her cat Cinnamon. I thought about the look on Travis's face when we mooned him, and about how Mom was right –

you have to wear clean underwear every day because you just never know.

I was about to drift off when I heard Nurse Opal from the other side of the door.

"Oh, hi. Nice to see you again. Dustin is doing just fine – and he's good to go."

Maybe Mom had brought me a dozen chocolate-covered cream-filleds to ease my suffering.

"I would ask that Dustin be examined by your family physician, though," Nurse Opal said. "Simply as a precautionary measure."

Oh, man!

"He's right in there."

Mom was going to be in one of her moods – not only for missing half a day's work, but for having to dish out money to see a doctor too. *I should sue Travis Buttrick.*

"Come on, Freakshow. Move it!"

It wasn't my mother standing in the doorway. It was my juvenile-delinquent brother, Gordy.

I should sue Mom.

Chapter 4

Double Take

Barf Breath got out of school an hour early on Fridays, making him the logical choice for chauffeur. The radio was busted, so the ride home in Gordy's rusty old make-out mobile was quiet – except that every time he hit a pothole, the tools in the trunk clattered and I moaned in pain. I think he did it on purpose, to torture me.

"Nice dice," I said, swatting the fuzzy pink blocks hanging off the rearview mirror.

"Keep your paws off 'em!" he snarled. "Those are antiques."

"Whatever you say, Elvis."

That crack got me a knuckle punch on the leg. I figured we were even.

Gordy had met his latest girlfriend, Sheila, at the new diner in town, the Jukebox Café. I guess she was heavy into the 50s, 'cause Big Brother had transformed himself into a full-fledged greaser: slicked-back hair, a tight white T-shirt.

There was even a pack of cigarettes rolled up in one of his sleeves. Gordy went through more girlfriends than Wally did cheeseburgers, and his "look" changed with every single girl. His annoying personality, however, was a permanent feature.

Gordy said only four more words to me for the rest of the trip home: "Are you wearing makeup?" It was a good thing I'd changed back into my pants.

Thanks to a little spit, Kleenex, and elbow grease, the red circles on my cheeks were gone by the time we pulled up to our house. The whole school must've gotten dismissed early, 'cause LMNOP was in her side yard, digging up dirt. (Yeah, us Buttermilk Fallians are a real classy bunch.) I pretended I didn't see her and sprinted up the porch steps. Mom was home from work already, and naturally Gordy couldn't wait to tell her what the nurse had said about my being examined by our physician – he knew I hated doctors. So Mom carted me off to the Claremont Clinic.

The doc was nice enough, but he kept saying stuff like "Did you get hit with a fastball, sport?" and "Take a nasty slide into home plate, slugger?" As if every boy my age was automatically a jock wannabe. Mom set him straight – sort of. "Dustin tripped on the playground and bonked his head on a flagpole."

Okay, I'd had to lie to her. Otherwise she would've shown up at school, seeking justice, and the subject of the play would've come up for sure. The doc finally said that everything checked out okay, but that I should take the next day off to rest. First I got excited, but then I realized the next day was Saturday. What a gyp!

But that was all "water under my bridgework," as Aunt Birdie would say. The next morning I was up at the crack of eleven. Just enough time to make a mad dash to the kitchen to grab some snacks before my favorite TV show came on.

"Uh-oh. Mom, what the heck are you doing?"

"What's it look like I'm doing?" she said, planting herself midsofa with a steaming cup of coffee in one hand and the remote control in the other. "It's time for my program."

"But *Double Take* is on! Why can't we have five televisions, like a normal family?"

Usually it was Gordy I had to fight with for control of the TV. Fortunately, he was already out with his psycho friends, probably plotting a rumble at the high-school hop. But in front of the TV set on Saturday morning was definitely a No-Mom Zone.

"Are you sure it's on now?" I whined. "What's the name of it?"

"I forget. It's on the Home Sweet Home Network."

"Not *Trash to Trendy!*" That's the show where they teach you stuff like how to make a fancy serving tray out of an old garbage-can lid. But no matter how many coats of gold paint or angel decals they cover it with, it still ends up looking like a garbage-can lid.

"No, a new one," Mom said. "A cooking show."

"Well, that's not gonna help – unless it's on the Miracle Network."

"Listen, it's not easy being thrown into the dating pool at my age," she said, searching through the channels. "And you know what they say: 'The quickest way to a man's heart is through his stomach.'"

"No offense, Mom, but find another route."

"Dustin!"

I felt bad about that as soon as I said it, but cooking wasn't one of Mom's strong points. And listening to her talk about dating made me itch. My aunts kept telling her to get on with her life, that it was high time. It did seem like Dad had been gone forever – but it had only been three years, if you're counting. He left us to be a stand-up comic. No joke. One weekend he had an out-of-town gig and didn't come back Sunday night. Or the night after that, or the night after that. He showed up a week later and things went back to normal, except with a lot more yelling between him and Mom. A few months after that he left for good. Whenever I get really angry about it, I force myself to think of the good times we had. I play those memories over and over again in my brain, like an old black-and-white movie.

"Your show's not even on, Mom," I said, lunging for the remote. "Turn it to channel twelve."

"Stop it!" she said, and clobbered me with a pillow.

"Oww, my lump!"

"Oh, I forgot," Mom said. "See what you made me do?" She gently pushed my hair back to examine my head. "So how're you feeling this morning? Better?"

"I guess," I said, looking up at her with hound-dog eyes.

"It looks like the lump has gone down. You have to stop being such a klutz."

A shuffling noise came from the kitchen.

"Knock-knock. Dorothy?"

We turned to see Granny Grubbs wearing a robe, slippers, and a plastic bubble cap, huffing and puffing her way through the living-room archway.

"Do you mind if I use your tub?" Granny asked.

"Umm – not at all," Mom said, sounding unsure. "Help yourself."

"I've been waiting all morning for Birdie to give herself a home perm so I could get in the bathroom for my ginger soak," Granny said. "You know, it helps when my arthritis flares up. Finally Miss America comes out and – whooey, I thought I'd pass out from the fumes! I don't know what kind of crazy chemicals they put in that concoction, but I'm not breathing them in."

As soon as the sound of running water was coming from the john, Mom whispered, "Now's a good time for me to go downstairs and start planning your gran's surprise birthday party with your aunts. So the TV is all yours, your highness."

She kissed my forehead, grabbed her coffee cup, and fled, saying, "Feet off the coffee table, mister."

We lived upstairs in a two-family home but spent a lot of our time downstairs, with my aunt Olive and my aunt Birdie and Granny Grubbs. I was the man of the house. (Gordy didn't count, 'cause he was a big flake and was hardly ever around.) Even though Mom wasn't a real Grubbs, my aunts and Granny had all pitched in to help her out since the divorce. Mom didn't have any blood relatives to turn to – her folks passed away years before I was even born.

Anyway, I was alone at last – sort of. I did a test run to make sure everything was in grabbing distance from the couch: half a box of assorted Jack Sprat doughnuts, a full box of Dino-S'mores cereal, a carton of milk, the remote control. My morning would be back on track with a single *click!*

You'll double over with laughter when Buddy uses his dad's hair-growing ointment to try to grow a beard on today's *hair*-larious episode of *Double Take!* Laugh-Fest Saturday Morning is brought to you by Keggler's Crustacean Crunch cereal.

"Wow, there's blueberry barnacles, chocolate clams, and marshmallow snails!"

"Turn that down," Granny yelled from the bathroom. "I can't hear myself think."

"Well, close the door, Gran!"

I didn't want to accidentally see her naked and be scarred for life.

Crustacean Crunch is fun to munch for breakfast, snacks, and even lunch. Arrrrgh!

I was singing along to the jingle with Pirate Pete when the phone rang. I picked it up and heard another *"Arrrrgh!"*

It was Wally, calling right on time. We were die-hard *Double Take* fans and had a pact to watch every episode together, even if we weren't in the same room. *Double Take* was about these twin brothers who were total opposites. Buddy was the cool brother and Bailey was the dork. The best part was that they were both played by the same actor – Jeremy Jason Wilder. The luckiest kid on the planet.

In our class, on Friday afternoons we had open discussion periods where Miss Honeywell would ask, "Okay, what do y'all wanna talk about today?" Wally and I would give each other two quick looks and shout, *"Double Take!"* Miss Honeywell never took us up on it.

"Hey, Wal, before I forget – you wanna come to my gran's birthday party? It's three weeks from today, the seventeenth. It's gonna be huge."

"Any food?"

"Tons."

"Do I have to bring a present?"

"Dunno. Probably."

"I'll get back to you on that," Wally said. "Oh, crud! This show's not another rerun, is it?"

"They're all reruns now. When's it gonna sink in?"

Double Take used to be on at eight o'clock on Thursday nights; then they stopped making new episodes and threw the reruns in with the Saturday morning cartoons. Not a good sign.

"It's the Follican one," I said.

"The what?"

"That stuff for bald guys." I chirped out another jingle. "'If your head can't grow it, Folli-*can!*'"

That's probably why I couldn't remember things like who Lewis and Clark were or what the capital of Pennsylvania is – too many jingles and sitcom plots were taking up valuable brain space.

"Oh, yeah. Buddy's head ends up looking like a giant egg-plant," Wally said. "So how's *your* head?"

"Fine."

"Quick, before it comes on, tell me again about the famous kid who's transferring into our class! What did the nurse say, exactly?"

"I already told you."

"Well, did she give you any hints, like –" Wally stopped talking and the sound got muffled. "Yeah, Ma? Okay, I'll ask him."

"Ask me what?" I said.

"My ma wants to know if you liked the costume she made you."

"Tell her yeah," I said. "And tell her not to mention it to my mom if she runs into her at the grocery store or anything. Tell her she's real sensitive about not knowing how to sew. She's probably better off not even knowing about the play at all."

I heard phone-fumbling.

"Dustin? It's Wallace's mom. Don't worry, I won't tell your mother about the play. We certainly don't want to hurt her feelings. I just hope I didn't work my fingers to the bone making all those costumes for nothing. You know Principal Futterman. He'll put the play off till kingdom come."

"No, we're definitely doing it, Mrs. Dorkin," I said. "We'd *better* be doing it!"

"All I know is, if it doesn't involve sports, that man can't be bothered," she said. "He postponed the PTA bake sale so long, we had to cancel it – and now I've got a pantry full of coconut-almond hockey pucks. Oh, he'd like that!"

"Ma, it's your own fault," I heard Wally say. "You know I can't stand coconut."

Just then, the front door flew open and Gordy oozed in, dragging Sheila – straight out of the 1950s and into our living room. She wasn't the poodle-skirt, ponytail variety I'd hoped for. More like a skanky greaser chick, with big hair, a pink leather jacket, and too much makeup.

"Where's Mom?" Gordy grunted.

"Downstairs," I said, putting my hand over the receiver.

Sheila perched on the arm of the couch next to me, picking something out of her teeth, while Gordy dumped half a box of Dino-S'mores into his mouth.

I hope he chokes on a stegosaurus.

"Gimme the phone," Gordy said.

"I'm using it!"

"I have to make a freakin' phone call," he said, ripping the receiver out of my hand. "It's important!"

He actually hung up on Wally's mom and started dialing. I grabbed the remote control and turned up the volume on the television.

"Turn that down," Gordy said.

"No can do. I'm watching *Double Take*. It's important."

"I thought they took that off the air," Sheila said.

"It's on Saturday mornings now," I told her.

"That show bites the big one," Gordy said. "And this Freakshow's got that Jeremy Jason Jerk's face plastered all over his room. I'm tellin' ya, there's something wrong with this kid." He thwacked my arm with the phone. "I said, turn it down!"

I turned up the volume as loud as it would go. Gordy dropped the phone, dived over the back of the couch, and torpedoed me.

"Hey, get off!" I yelled.

"Leave him alone, Gordo," Sheila said. "Jeez, don't be such a drag."

"Yeah, Gordo!"

He was strangling my wrist to get the remote control when I pulled his T-shirt sleeve and saw a flash of orange on his upper arm. In the middle of our struggle I got a better look and made out some sort of burning skull.

"Is that – that's not a tattoo, is it?" I said, surrendering the remote. "That better not be a real one, or Mom'll kill you."

He pushed me away and tossed the remote to Sheila, who clicked the TV on mute and started channel surfing.

"So what if it's real?" Gordy said, picking up the phone. "It's my body. I'm old enough to do what I want."

While he was dialing, I edged in a little closer to him, trying to make out the scabby letters under the skull.

"Uh-huh," he mumbled into the receiver, slicking back his greasy hair. "Partly cloudy . . . a high of sixty-seven . . . winds from the west-northwest gusting to – blah, blah, blah . . . humidity, thirty-nine percent. See, babe – no rain till tomorrow."

"*That* was your important phone call?" I said, but he ignored me.

"Come on," he said to Sheila, "let's rock 'n' roll."

"Hey," I said, "what's R-E-B-U-L stand for?"

"*Rebel,* you loser."

"You're the loser," I said. "*Rebel* is spelled with an *e,* not a u." All of a sudden it hit me and I burst out laughing. "Omigod! You have to walk around for the rest of your life with a typo on your arm!"

Gordy did an all-out attack on me, twisting my arm behind my back and yelling, "Take it back, take it back," like it was my fault. Real mature.

"Aw, leave the kid alone," Sheila muttered. "*American Graffiti* is on. I love this movie."

When the pain outweighed the laughter, I "took it back" and curled up in the corner of the couch. I knew I didn't have a snowball's chance in h-e-double-hockey-sticks of getting back control of the TV set as long as Elvis and Priscilla were in the room. Luckily, it was the last twenty minutes of the movie.

When it ended, Gordy pointed his finger at my face and warned, "You'd better keep your big mouth shut about the tattoo, see? 'Cause I've got some juicy dirt on you too." Then he grabbed his main squeeze and my box of doughnuts and bolted.

I was stunned for a few seconds, wondering if Gordy really knew something – or if he was just being the usual Gordy. When I switched channels on the TV, the *Double Take* credits were already rolling.

See ya next week, kids. Same time, same place — brand-new show!

"New show?" I said back to the TV. "What about *Double Take?*"

You'll slap yourself silly if you miss it when the *Maniac Muldoon* cartoon makes its hilarious debut on Laugh-Fest Saturday Morning!

Wally called again. Our conversation started out just like the one before.

"Arrrrgh!"

Chapter 5

Water Balloons

Wally's mom had me all worried for nothing. Monday morning, after the Pledge of Allegiance, Futterman announced that *The Castle of the Crooked Crowns* would be performed in a special assembly at one o'clock that Thursday – April Fools' Day! We rehearsed like crazy for three days, and I knew my lines (and everyone else's) backward and forward. But come Wednesday night I was so wound up, I must've slept maybe five minutes. Tops.

When the big day finally arrived, Miss Honeywell was as dressed up as I'd ever seen her, in a silky yellow dress with a matching jacket. Maybe it was just the sun streaking in, but I swear she was glowing like an angel dropped from heaven – only in high heels and with a big hairdo.

"Good morning, class," she said. "Well, we've certainly got an exciting day ahead of us!"

I'll say. It felt as if water balloons were sloshing around in my stomach all morning.

"I have a bit of news," Miss Honeywell said, sitting on the edge of her desk. She crossed her legs, with a shoe dangling off one foot. If I weren't a nervous wreck I might've drooled. "I'm not exactly sure why the main office wanted to keep all the details hush-hush," she said. "I mean, y'all were going to find out eventually. But that transfer student I told you about will not be joining our class next week, as expected."

The famous kid? No way.

"He's arriving today!" Miss Honeywell said, so excited that she kicked off her shoe.

Who starts at a new school in April, anyway? Why bother? And what are the odds that he'd get here on Play Day, of all days?

"I should explain that this young man is very – well, let's say 'special,'" she said, hopping down from the desk and stepping into her shoe. "Not to say that y'all aren't special, because you know I think each one of you is finer than hair on a frog. But he's special in – well, a very special way."

Huh? If I didn't know better, I'd swear she was drunk.

"Now I want you to treat him just like you'd treat anybody else," she said. "The last thing in the world we want to do is to make him feel uncomfortable."

Millicent Fleener raised her hand.

"Yes, Millicent?"

"Is he physically challenged? Like, in a wheelchair or something?"

"No, he's not," Miss Honeywell said.

Darlene Deluca's hand went up, but she didn't wait to get called on.

"Is he from another country and doesn't speak English?"

"No."

Wally's desk was right next to mine. His hand shot up next. "Ooh, ooh, ooh!" he said, bouncing up and down like his seat was on fire and he was putting it out with his rear end.

"Yes?"

"Is he, like, forty-five years old and just now coming back to school to finish his education?"

The class groaned.

"It's possible," Wally said. "Stuff like that happens all the time."

"It does not," I whispered. "And I already told you he was somebody *famous!*"

"So? You could be forty-five and famous."

"Y'all are getting carried away now," Miss Honeywell said, fiddling with her charm bracelet. "You'll find out, all in good time. Just remember to be yourselves. It's no big deal."

She was right. It wasn't a big deal – it was a gi-normous deal! When Reggie MacPherson transferred into our class, Miss Honeywell barely mentioned anything about it. She just made sure there was an empty desk ready and waiting. But today our classroom was hospital clean: the windows and blackboards were washed, the papers on the bulletin boards were lined up perfectly, and there were even fresh flowers on her desk. *Jeez, who is this kid? The heir to the throne of Bulgaria?*

There was a loud knock on our door. I thought it was the Crown Prince for sure, but then Futterman's big head appeared on the other side of the glass. He waggled his finger for Miss Honeywell to join him in the hall.

"I'll be right back," she said, smoothing her hair on her way to the door. "In the meantime, get out your history books and turn to chapter twelve. Y'all can get a head start on your reading assignment for tonight."

Fair enough. I cracked open my book and began reading.

> The earliest castles were made of wood and first appeared in Britain sometime after 1066, when William the Conqueror won the Battle of Hastings. . . .

I had "reflector brain." That's when you keep reading the same sentence over and over but the words don't sink in. That's when you keep reading the same sentence over and over but the words don't sink in. (Kidding.)

I tried to catch a glimpse of what was happening in the hall, but I couldn't see much from my seat. Futterman and Miss Honeywell were probably discussing where to roll out the red carpet for the new kid. I looked up at the clock. Three hours and forty-five minutes until showtime. I could feel those water balloons expanding with every *tick, tick, tick*. Then my stomach gurgled so loudly that heads popped up from their books. It was like the Battle of Hastings was being reenacted in my intestines.

Miss Honeywell swept back into the room with a thick manila folder and sat at her desk.

"Excuse me, Miss Honeywell, but what about the play?" Darlene asked. "I mean, it's still scheduled for today after lunch, right?"

"Right," Miss Honeywell said.

"Well, can we do a quick line-through right now? Just so we don't forget anything?"

"Oh, we're in good shape," Miss Honeywell said, leafing through the folder. "There is such a thing as being over-rehearsed. Let's just continue with our quiet time – but you may review your lines individually if you wish."

She filed the folder in her bottom drawer, removed a tiny mirror, and dug out some makeup crud from the corners of her eyes. Then she got up and straightened the stacks of paper next to the computers – three times. When she sat down again, she couldn't stop staring at the door.

I was beginning to think that Miss Honeywell didn't give a squat about the play anymore. She was all wigged out because this new kid was coming.

"Dustin?" she said in a half whisper. "Dustin Grubbs?"

Okay, maybe I was wrong. Maybe it was time for her to

consult with her top-notch assistant director to go over some last-minute production notes.

"Yes?" I answered.

"Would you be a peach and lower the shade on the window next to you? The sun is blinding the fourth row."

That was *his* row – the famous kid's row.

"Yes, ma'am."

I whipped down the shade in one quick jerk and shot her a look of deep concern with a hint of disappointment. She just smiled and fluffed her peonies.

I didn't get it. Weren't there lighting and sound cues to go over? Sets and costumes to be checked? Fire alarms to be dismantled? I mean, I love you, Miss Honeywell, but get with the program.

When I sat back down, the water balloons in my stomach had reached their breaking point.

"Excuse me, Miss Honeywell?" I said, raising my hand.

"Yes, Dustin? What is it?"

"I – I don't think I'm feeling very well."

"What's wrong?"

"I feel kinda queasy. Can I – *may* I please use the restroom?" (Good English in the middle of a crisis. Major points.)

"Why, of course," Miss Honeywell said. "You do look flushed." A sudden look of horror flashed across her face. "You're not going to throw up, are you?"

I think she was more worried about my messing up her

spick-and-span classroom and spoiling the Boy Wonder's arrival than she was about my health.

"Uh – I'm not sure," I said, wiping the sweat off my forehead.

Now the whole class looked worried. See, Brian Flabner threw up the week before, and it still smelled a little. Ever since then Miss Honeywell had had to keep the back window open a few inches. She told us that if we felt the urge, we didn't have to wait for permission to go to the bathroom, that we should just run. That's powerful stuff.

"It's probably a case of the jitters," Miss Honeywell said. "Take the hall pass from the cabinet. Do you want someone to go with you?"

"No, thanks. I'm good."

Twenty-three pairs of anxious eyes followed me around the room. When I opened the cabinet door, I noticed that the entire row next to me was leaning in the opposite direction.

Chapter 6

Stalled

I flashed my wooden pass to the hall monitor sitting at the desk near the water fountain. It turned out to be Public Enemy Number One – Travis Buttrick. He grabbed my pass and examined it like he was White House security. I think he wanted me to get a load of his flashy new scuba-diving watch – like I cared. Like he *really* needed it to go skinny-dipping in Buttermilk Creek. Travis handed the pass back and I flew toward the bathroom.

"Hey, no running in the halls, Grubbs!"

"Sorry."

"And by the way, can I pleeeeze have your autograph, O great *actor?*"

I should've turned around and punched him, but I just kept walking. I didn't want to wind up in the nurse's office again with a lumpy head. Not today, of all days.

The boys' bathroom was dimly lit and had bars on the windows, like something out of a prison movie. The smell of radioactive pine cleanser was so strong it stung your eyes. And there was the added stink of cigarette smoke. Wally said there was a gang of eighth-grade criminals who cut class and hung out there, but I'd never seen them.

I splashed some cold water on my face from the only faucet that worked, wiped my hands on my pants, and went into the only stall that had a door. I guess the school didn't trust boys with hot water, paper towels, and closed stalls.

"Your *wish* is my command, Princess." I sat there, trying out different line readings. "Your wish *is* my command, Princess. Your wish is my *command*, Princess."

"Dustin?"

"Is that the Walrus? I'm behind door number one."

"You're not barking turkeys in there, are you?"

"What?"

"Barfing up road pizza?"

"No. I'm feeling a little better."

"Good," Wally said. "Miss Honeywell sent me to check on the teacher's pet. And stop calling me Walrus – I'm a serious musician, remember?"

"Yeah, whatever. Hey, somebody drew a picture of Futterman in here, with bolts through his neck."

"Really? Let me see. I'm sick of talking to the door."

"Your wish is my command."

I tried to slide the metal lock on the stall door, but it didn't budge.

"Hey, I think this thing's stuck."

"Oh, come on," Wally said. "This is a joke, right?"

I tried the lock again, but it wasn't going anywhere.

"No, I'm serious."

I rattled it; I pounded it; I banged on it with my wooden pass. Nothing. I searched my pockets for something that could help me, but all I came up with was a small piece of paper that said "Inspected by #2784," a bubblegum cigar, and a red pen. I jammed the pen point next to the metal bar in the lock and pushed it as hard as I could. That turned out to be a stupid idea, 'cause the pen broke and my hands got stained with ink.

This was turning into a 911 moment. The stall door was ancient – way too tall to climb, and there were only about five inches of space at the bottom. Not enough room for even a skinny sixth-grader to squash through. I was stuck – and stuck bad.

"Stand back!" Wally said.

"What are you going to do? Don't be an idiot!"

I pressed my face up to the slit at the edge of the door, closed one eye, and peeked through. Wally was backing up and building up steam, like a bull ready to charge.

"Just staaaand back!" he yelled.

"Where? The toilet's in the way!"

I hopped up on the toilet and braced myself against the wall.

Fwump!

"Ow!"

Fwump!

"Oww!"

He kept ramming the door with all his might, but the door was mightier.

"Wally, stop! That only works in the movies."

Fwump!

"*Owww!* It's Wallace!"

I'm trapped like a rat, and he's worried about being called Wallace! We kicked the door from both sides like maniacs, but I figured we'd better stop before one of us broke a toe.

"This isn't working." *There's no way the play is going to be canceled again because of something this stupid!* I didn't want to have to say it, but: "You'd better go tell Miss Honeywell. Try to be –"

"What's going on in here?"

That voice sounded familiar. It was either God or the principal.

"Dustin is stuck in the stall, Mr. Futterman. Uh, he can't get out."

"I smell cigarette smoke. You boys weren't smoking in here,

were you?" Futterman's deep voice ricocheted off the tile walls. He was a gigantic man with a Frankenstein-shaped head – just like in the graffiti – and was bald as a bowling ball.

"No, sir," Wally replied, "we never smoke in here. Or anywhere. We don't smoke. Someone must've been smoking, 'cause I can smell it too, but it wasn't us, I swear!"

Wally can't stop blabbering when he's nervous, and it makes him look guilty even if he's not. But who could blame him? Futterman could make a snowman sweat.

"I can't get out, Mr. Futterman," I said. "The lock is stuck."

"Did you try jiggling it?"

If anybody had walked in right then and heard that question, I would've croaked.

"I tried everything, sir."

The stall door rattled a few times, and then there was a final *thump*.

"I'll get a janitor," Mr. Futterman said. "Don't move!"

"Don't move"? How did he get to be principal, anyway?

"Walrus? Wally? Wallace, are you still there?" No answer. I sat down, peeled back the cellophane from my bubblegum cigar, and tried to suck out any nutrients. I needed energy to think.

The lunch bell rang. Time flies when you're having fun. I could hear chattering and locker-slamming echoing through the halls. It wasn't long before voices filled the bathroom. I hugged my legs to my chest to hide my telltale feet.

Knock, knock, knock!

"Dustball, we know you're in there!"

"Hey, Dustin, did ya fall in?"

"What's the matter? Can't you *act* your way out?"

Wally must've blurted out to the whole class that I was stuck in the bathroom stall! My brain was frozen, and I couldn't think of a single snappy comeback. That wasn't like me.

"Dustin, hon, are you all right?" It was Miss Honeywell. "The gentleman from Maintenance is here to rescue you."

Kill me now.

The janitor slipped a little can of something under the stall and told me to spray it onto the lock. It smelled like gasoline, and it took only a few squirts for the bolt to slide right out. I hesitated. The only way to escape total humiliation would be to go straight for the laugh. I crossed my eyes, wiggled my cigar, and kicked the door open, shouting, "April Fools'!"

I couldn't believe it. My whole class was crammed into the boys' john, with Futterman and Miss Honeywell standing front and center. And right next to them, laughing and clapping with the rest of my class, was a kid I saw every day on posters, T-shirts, and the TV screen: the star of *Double Take,* my favorite sitcom of all time – *the* Jeremy Jason Wilder!

Chapter 7

The Castle of the Crooked Crowns

Many sunrises ago, in the Land of Galico,
On a warm and dewy, bright September morn,
There arose unbounded bliss, unimagined happiness,
For the daintiest of princesses was born.

In that very castle too, in a room without a view,
Came a heartfelt but uncelebrated joy,
With a caterwauling wail, looking freckle-faced and frail,
Sprang the Jester's brand-new bouncing baby boy.

Cynthia Zimmerman – the Minstrel – finished her opening song in front of the curtain. I was behind the proscenium, smashed up against Leonard Shempski, the techie, who smelled like old cheese and pencils. One thought kept running through my head: *I'm freakin' out! I'm freakin' out!*

Not only had I just met Jeremy Jason Wilder face to face, and not only was he going to be in my class – but he was actually sitting out there in the audience, watching *me* try to do what *he* did best.

If this is all some weird dream, now would be the perfect time to wake up.

I gave myself a pinch. Okay, not a dream. Leonard hit play on the tape recorder for the first two sound effects: Loud Slap and Baby's Cry. That was Cynthia's cue to start narrating.

"From the moment they took their first steps together, Princess Precious and Jingle Jangles, the Jester's son, were inseparable."

"Louder!" I said. Cynthia's voice had a habit of trailing off.

"Were inseparable," she repeated.

I pulled Pepper onto the dark stage for our opening pose. My heart was thumping up a storm.

"They spent hours frolicking in the Royal Sniffing Gardens," Cynthia went on, "and playing games like ring-around-the-dragon and pin-the-tail-on-the-unicorn."

"Do good," Pepper whispered to me. I squeezed her sweaty hand.

"Pull the curtains!" I called to Leonard. "Now!"

The opening curtains screeched like a howler monkey, but the audience applauded when they saw the set. So far, so good. My mind was still on Jeremy, though, sitting out there, watching – just like a regular person. I couldn't breathe for a second, until I crammed the thought down to the bottom of my brain. (Did I mention that I was freaking out?)

"Do tell me another joke, Jingle Jangles!" Pepper said.

"Your wish is my command, Princess," I said, with a sweeping bow. "Umm, let's see. How do you make a gooseberry float?"

"I haven't a clue," Pepper said. "How *do* you make a gooseberry float?"

"Take one gooseberry" – I did a forward somersault – "and toss it in the moat!"

The audience groaned. With the spotlight blinding me, they looked like a giant black blob.

"Oh, Jing," Pepper said, giggling. "I believe each joke you tell is funnier than the last."

"It's all in the timing," I said, hopping to my feet. "I frequently work on timing with my frather – *father*."

Ugh! A flub already? Maybe wearing Dad's neckties as a belt is bringing me bad luck.

"Another," Pepper said, jumping up and down. "Tell another!"

"As you wish. But promise me that I shan't be thrown in the dungeon if you split your royal sides."

"I promise."

"Okay, then, brace yourself. Why did the peahen cross the road? . . ."

After the scene ended, I had a few minutes offstage to ditch the belt and pull myself together. The spotlight shot across the stage, past Cynthia, to the exit sign, then back to Cynthia.

"The years flew by faster than a griffin's gallop," she said, "and by the time they turned thirteen, Princess Precious and Jingle Jangles were gazing at each other with a special glint in their eyes. Alas, they were falling in love."

A rowdy *oooh* came out of the audience, followed by a *shhh*.

"It was important, however, that the Princess marry well. For you see," Cynthia said, cupping her hand to her cheek, "despite their enviable bloodline and noble airs, the royal family was poor."

"Louder!" I said.

"Dirt poor!" she said, shooting me a nasty look. "In fact, their silken robes were fraying at the edges, and their crowns were dented and sat crookedly upon their regal heads."

The spotlight zigzagged across the stage and landed on Darlene as the Royal Nanny and Wally as the King.

"I'm trrrroubled, Your Highness," Darlene said, swishing her dress. "Your daughter is spending entirely too much time with the fool's son and far too little time on her embrrrroidery."

She was doing a bad English accent, which Miss Honey-well had told her *not* to do, and was rolling her *r*'s.

"But, Lady Pickerel," Wally said in his deep King voice, "my daughter cherishes her afternoons with young Jingle Jangles. Why, she seems to blossom in his very presence!"

"My point prrrrecisely," Darlene snarled. "And no good

can come of it. Besides, it seems that your Pr*rrr*ecious has unknowingly captured the heart of a pr*rrr*ince! *Rrrr*umor has it that Kr*rrr*ispen of Kaloo rides past our gardens every fortnight to catch a mere glimpse of her."

I popped my head up from behind the castle wall with a look of utter despair. That's what it said in the stage directions: [Utter despair].

"Why, such a union could save our entire kingdom!" Wally was stroking his fake beard with one hand and undoing the Velcro on his costume with the other. "But I shall not compromise my daughter's happiness."

I popped back down. It had never occurred to me before how lame this play really was. Jeremy must be snoring by now. Why did Miss Honeywell have to pick such a dorky play?

" 'Tis hardly a compromise," Darlene said. "The Pr*rrr*ince is fair of face, and sweet words are said to flow like honey from his lips."

*She's pr*rrr*actically singing her lines. C'mon, pick up the pace, people!*

"Perhaps we should invite him to our midsummer festival," Wally said as they headed offstage.

"Forgive me, Your Majesty, but what midsummer festival?"

"Exactly. Make the arrangements at once!"

As soon as they hit the wings, Wally started changing into a different costume. I guess he was determined to work in all five his mom had made, or die trying.

Cynthia droned on with her boring narration; the lords and ladies did their circle dance, which looked more like medieval bumper cars. I couldn't wait until my next scene so I could liven things up.

Enter the Prince to a fanfare of – *crickets? Leonard is so dead!* Felix Plunket really looked the part: tall, skinny, blond hair, blue eyes. He hit his mark center stage and stood tall, with his hands planted firmly on his hips.

"Welcome to Galico!" I said, cartwheeling onto the stage. "Lengthy journey, my lord? If you don't mind my saying so, Your Majesty looks a tad weary. And your fine robes smell – well, like the insides of a sick goat."

That got a laugh. Jeremy, did you catch that?

"I'm afraid I'm the bearer of some unfortunate news for Your Princeliness. Let me see, how can I put this delicately?" I said, scratching my hat. "You're late!"

I sang my little song, dancing a lively jig around Felix.

The festival is ending now,
The mead is drunk; we ate the cow,
It seems your trip was made in vain,
So, on your horse and back again!

Felix stood taller, looking even more princely, and stared into the audience.

Jeez, he's really milking it.

"So, on your horse and back again!" I repeated.

Nothing. He wasn't acting – he was panicking! I tried to feed him his line without moving my lips.

"Be. Gone. You. Oaf."

"B-b-b-buh . . ."

His stutter kicked in, and a sweat ball dripped off the tip of his nose. Now *I* was panicking!

"I know what you're thinking," I said, wiggling my fingers in his face. "'Be gone, you oaf! Or you'll squash me like a caterpillar!'"

"Young fool, away!" Wally shouted, stomping onto the stage. "That is not the proper way to greet a prince."

Saved by the Walrus. He had on a red tunic with brown spots. His mom must've reworked his pepperoni-pizza costume from last Halloween.

"A thousand pardons, Your Highness," I said, "but I –"

"Hold your tongue, Dustin!"

"What?"

"I meant, Jingle Jangles."

Wally started cracking up. I socked him in one of the pepperonis.

"Oww! What'd you do that for?"

"And ten-times-a-thousand pardons to you, Prince Krispen," I said to Felix, who was starting to wobble. Some Prince.

"The Jester's son is high spirited but surely meant no harm,"

Wally said, strolling downstage. "Your visit to my kingdom is most welcome indeed."

As if things weren't going badly enough, I noticed that the back of Wally's tunic was tucked into the elastic band of his tights. And his dinosaur underpants were showing through!

"Allow me to reveal our most magnificent sights!" he said, bowing low to Felix.

The audience roared.

I said my next line staring at the floor so I wouldn't lose it. When I looked up, Wally was gone. Right in the middle of the scene!

Now it was just me and the petrified Prince again – and a packed house, with Jeremy sitting out there, laughing with the rest of them, and not in a good way. After a pause you could drive a truck through, someone from the audience started tossing pennies at us. I wanted to exit stage left and just keep running. But I decided to wing it.

"Since Your Highness insists, I shall summon the Princess at once! Princess Precious!" I shouted, running upstage. "You have company. Wherefore art thou, Princess? Come out, come out, wherever you are!"

The backdrop rippled.

"I'm coming!" Pepper shouted. "Hold your horses!"

I heard running footsteps, then *rip!* – Pepper came busting through the middle of the paper drawbridge, leaving a giant hole just like in the Road Runner cartoons.

"Gentle Princess," I said, clutching her arm, "I'm sorry to have awakened you from your royal nap."

"Huh?" she said with her eyes closed. "Is that in the script?"

Before I could get another word out, there was a loud *crack!* I looked at Felix to see if he'd broken in half, but he was still rock solid. Pepper must've knocked a wooden support loose.

Leonard hollered, "Heads up!" A scream came from stage right. I looked up and saw the tall flat with the tower painted on it toppling over.

I grabbed Pepper with one hand, Felix with the other, and ran across the stage, shouting, "Twister! Run for your royal lives!"

Trumpets blared, horses whinnied, crickets chirped, babies cried. And the audience howled.

The collapsing flat took another one with it, barely missing us. I pushed Pepper out of the way but slammed into the flagpole stage right. It knocked the giant speaker off the wall, and then *boom!* – the speaker smashed through the top of the baby-grand piano. The tremendous sound of piano strings vibrating shook the auditorium. Shook my bones.

"Curtain!" I cried. "Pull the curtain!" But Leonard was gone. I threw myself onto the ropes and yanked with all my might.

"Wait!" Wally said, zooming toward the stage. "Just two seconds!"

I wasn't waiting for anything. I just kept pulling. But I

couldn't pull fast enough to hide what was happening center stage: Wally was standing on a pile of rubble, bowing. He was wearing costume number four (a zebra-print rug?). One final tug and the curtains were closed.

It was over.

Backstage was a disaster area. Four girls were crying, Felix was kicking the wall, and Pepper was screaming at Darlene.

"This is all your fault! The hot lights melted that eyelash adhesive. I told you not to use so much!"

"I didn't use any at all!" Darlene snapped. "I ran out, so I used rubber cement."

Miss Honeywell appeared, looking crazed.

"Is everyone all right?"

"Yeah," Darlene said.

"Speak for yourself!" Pepper hollered.

"Pepper, darlin', your eyes are all swollen!" Miss Honeywell said. "Darlene, please accompany her to the nurse's office. Everyone else, collect your belongings and proceed back to the classroom immediately."

The backstage door slammed.

"When I get my hands on – that was the biggest fiasco I have ever –"

It was Principal Futterman, too hot to finish a sentence.

"Now take it easy, Dan," Miss Honeywell said. "The good news is, no one got seriously hurt."

Futterman went ballistic, but I tuned out the yelling – just like when Mom and Dad were at each other's throats. I started going around collecting all the loose change that the mean kids had thrown on the stage.

Too bad Jeremy Jason Wilder had to sit through that disaster. I'll bet any money he switches to homeschooling after this. Hmm, eight cents and one Canadian nickel.

It's funny, this was my first paid performance, in a way. My first professional gig. That's Dad's word – *gig.*

"– and someone is going to be held accountable!"

The door slammed again, and when I turned around everyone was gone – except for Wally, who was sucking the cream out of a Twinkie.

"We should get back to class," he said. "The play went well, don't ya think?"

"What?"

"Well, the audience liked it."

"I can't believe you!" I buried my head in my hands.

"Why?" he said. "Oh. Sorry. Did you want a bite?"

Chapter 8

As Good as It Gets

"Everybody up!" Mom said, ripping my covers off. I didn't budge. "Come on, sleepyhead, you're going to be late for school."

"No, I'm not," I mumbled into my pillow, "'cause I'm not going."

"But you love school. And it's Friday – no phys ed. Just one more day till the weekend." She tickled the bottoms of my feet. It didn't work.

"Mommm!" I croaked. "Stop it."

"Okay, now you're going to make me late for work. You're not sick, are you?"

"Yes. No. Maybe. It depends on how you define *sick*."

"Come on, Dustin, I don't have time for this. If you're sick, I'm taking you to the doctor; if you're not sick, you're going to school. Pick one."

Tough choice, but school won out. Luckily, having a real, live TV star inches away from us in class seemed to wipe the play out of everyone's memories. Jeremy Jason Wilder looked just as he did on TV – same blue-black hair and dark eyes, maybe a little taller, and definitely thinner. I guess the camera really does add ten pounds. At lunchtime I expected a stretch limo to arrive and whisk him away, but he sat all by himself in the cafeteria, pretending to be a normal kid. No bodyguard. No bottled water. Not even dark sunglasses.

Pepper was wearing her sunglasses, though, 'cause she still had raccoon eyes from the rubber-cement incident. She was sitting with me and the Walrus, one table away from Jeremy. We were all playing it ultracool. But trying to ignore Jeremy was like trying to ignore a polka-dotted hippopotamus twirling fire batons. Wally decided to use his spoon as a mirror to follow his every move. Nobody dared cross the line and actually speak to Jeremy, though – that is, until Darlene came clomping in, wearing high heels and makeup.

"Hi, I'm Darlene," she said, dropping her tray down on Jeremy's table. "You're in my class."

"Jeremy."

"I know. I mean, who doesn't? I mean, it's nice to meet you." She was batting her eyelashes so fast you'd think she was trying to keep her eyeballs from falling out. "Mind if I sit?"

Darlene pulled up a chair without waiting for an answer.

"Well, if motormouth could talk to him, we could too," Wally said. "Come on!"

He and Pepper grabbed their trays, turned their chairs around, and scooted in next to Darlene. I stayed put and pretended to be absorbed in *New Horizons in Environmental Science, Level D*. But I tuned in to every little sound and move that was happening at the next table.

"Hey, Jeremy!" Wally said. "*Double Take* is my favorite show! Well, *was* my favorite show. I've seen every episode at least three times."

"Introduce yourself, ignoramus," Darlene said.

"Oh, sorry. Wallace P. Dorkin. This here's Pepper."

"Howdy," she said, peeking over her shades.

"Hi," Jeremy said.

"You must be, like, a millionaire, right? Do you have your own private jet?" Wally asked, shoveling coleslaw into his mouth. "Do you get to fly it?"

"You're not supposed to ask money questions," Darlene said, punching Wally's arm. "What's wrong with you?"

"No planes, no yachts, no race cars – yet," Jeremy said. "A lot of my money's tied up in some special account, and I don't get to see it until I'm, like, eighteen."

"Bummer!" Wally said, pounding the table so hard the trays rattled.

A hysterical third-grader wearing nothing but pink ran up

to their table. "Omigod! Do you know who you are?" she gushed. "I love you, Jeremy. No, you don't understand. I really *looove* you!" She dug a marker out of her pencil case and handed it to him. "Sign my arm, pleeeze? I swear I'll never wash it off."

As soon as he signed her arm, she screamed bloody murder and four of her friends stormed Jeremy, holding out assorted body parts for him to autograph.

"Okay, that's it!" Darlene barked. "This table is for sixthgraders only. So just move along quickly and nobody gets hurt."

"That's something I'll never get used to," Jeremy said, watching the squealing girls run back to their table. "Just imagine walking into a room and total strangers are falling all over themselves just 'cause you're you."

"I can relate," Darlene said, propping her head on her hand.

"So, tell me, Jer," Pepper said, "why would anyone in their right mind move from Hollywood to Buttermilk Falls?"

"Were you friends with any big-time movie stars out there?" Wally asked.

"One question at a time," Darlene said.

Jeremy emptied the last of his trail mix into his mouth and crumpled the bag. Darlene's hand snuck over and grabbed it. She was probably planning to auction it off on the Internet.

"After my series ended," Jeremy said, "the parental units decided we needed to get away from all the craziness of Tinseltown. That's why we moved here. They want me to have a little taste of normal."

Pepper was in sunglasses, chewing on her calluses, Darlene was dressed like someone's mother, and Wally was licking the sandwich he'd made out of fish sticks and potato chips. If Jeremy was looking for normal, he'd come to the wrong place.

"So, what street do you live on?" Wally asked.

"Come on, man, I can't tell you that," Jeremy said, brushing his hair back. "It's just outside of Butterfat Falls, okay?"

"Hey, Dustin!" Pepper said, throwing a cherry tomato at me. "Are you antisocial? Get over here already."

I choked on my chocolate milk. Part of me wanted to meet Jeremy face to face more than anything, and part of me – the bigger part – wanted to bury my head in my mashed potatoes. *With any luck maybe he won't recognize me.* I picked up my tray and took the long haul over to the next table.

"Here comes your biggest fan!" Wally said, all excited. "Jeremy, Dustin. Dustin, Jeremy. Dustin wants to be an actor too."

Wally was officially dead meat.

"Hey," I said, sliding into a chair.

"Hey," he said back.

A giggle erupted from another gaggle of little girls, who were hovering next to Jeremy, staring holes through him.

"Jeez," Darlene said. "Take a picture – it'll last longer."

One of them actually did.

"Darn paparazzi!" Darlene said.

Travis (wanna-see-a) Buttrick appeared out of nowhere, snatched the girl's disposable camera, and held it high over his head.

"Give it back, jerk-o!" the girl yelled, reaching for it.

"Just say the word, Jeremy," Travis said, ignoring her, "and I expose all her film."

"No, don't," Jeremy said. "I don't mind the pictures."

"You sure?"

Jeremy nodded. Travis tossed the camera back to the girl, who was close to tears, and she and her friends disappeared.

"I'm Travis," he said, extending his hand to Jeremy. They shook. I shuddered. "Anybody else give you any trouble, just let me know. I got your back, man."

Travis swaggered away, surveying the lunchroom as if he were Jeremy's official bodyguard.

"Don't let him fool you. Travis is a dirtbag," Darlene said, covering her leftover fish bits with napkins. "Now, what were we talking about before we were so rudely interrupted?"

"About how Dustin wants to be an actor too," Pepper said. "So, you're a pro, Jer. What'd you think of him in the play? I mean, before the set caved in and everything."

I knew she meant well, but Pepper was dead meat too.

"You were good," Jeremy said, looking me right in the face.

"Huh?"

"In that play. I thought you were good."

"Oh." My heart hiccuped. "Thanks."

Sure, he was forced into an answer – but he didn't say "you weren't bad" or "you were pretty good." He said *"good"!* A solid compliment. *The* Jeremy Jason Wilder, international celebrity, said I was good! And international celebrities must know what they're talking about.

"If you have any questions about acting or anything," Jeremy said, "just ask."

Was he kidding? I had tons. It was funny, though – I couldn't think of a single one. Still, I didn't want the lunch hour to end. I wanted to kick back, chew on a pretzel rod, and talk shop with my good pal Jeremy.

All of a sudden, a steel vise clamped down on my left shoulder.

"Mr. Grubbs. Come see me in my office after school. We need to talk."

Fee-Fi-Fo Futterman. His monster hand had probably left a permanent imprint.

The wooden bench outside the principal's office was big and hard, built just to make people sweat. It was working. I zeroed in on the doorknob, waiting for it to turn, dreading walking into that room "where seldom was heard an encouraging word." I had to snap out of it or I might spontaneously combust. Fortunately, I was an expert at getting my mind to switch topics at will.

I opened my spiral notebook, printed the word *good,* and turned the *o*'s into doughnuts. Then I began sketching banner designs for Granny Grubbs's upcoming seventy-fifth birthday bash. I remembered what Mom had said about inviting only one guest each. "All of our relatives are coming, and we can't afford to feed them plus the entire neighborhood." I knew Wally was going to be my one guest, because he was my best friend and – well, it was always Wally. But I couldn't help thinking how cool it'd be if I could invite Jeremy instead:

"So, who'd you invite to the party?" someone would ask.

"Oh, just a friend. Jeremy."

"Jeremy who?"

"Jeremy Jason Wilder."

"Not the TV star! You know him?"

"We hang out," I'd say. *"It's no big deal."*

Plus, a celeb at the party might distract my distant relatives from bombarding Mom with snide remarks and dirty looks because of the divorce and everything. I mean, they're all Dad's blood relations, and Mom isn't really a Grubbs anymore – only in name. But there's *no way* I could ever invite Jeremy. And there's no way he'd ever come. Not in a million years. Not in a kazillion-trillion –

"Come in, Mr. Grubbs."

Futterman held the door open and ushered me into – Jock World. The walls were covered with banners and plaques, and the shelves were crammed with trophies for every sport known to man. A signed baseball in a Plexiglas box sat at the front of his desk, and next to it was a framed photo of Futterman with his arm around a tiny blond lady and two boys with basketball-size heads.

"Jeez," I said. "You've won a ton of awards."

"Well, I've lived a lot of years, and I love sports," Futterman said. "Baseball especially. I was in the minors, you know. Probably could've made it into the major leagues, but I got a groin injury that ended my career."

"Sorry," I said, trying not to crack up at "groin injury."

"But that's all ancient history." He dropped his friendly tone. "We have some serious business to discuss. There's the matter of the damaged piano in the auditorium, for starters," he said, folding his arms. "We had it assessed, and the cost to repair it is astronomical. Certainly not in the school's budget – especially with the damage control we're doing after that grease fire in the cafeteria. Now, I know you weren't directly responsible for the state of the piano, but since it *was* a result of your little play, I'm holding you and Miss Honeywell accountable. So far she hasn't been able to offer any viable solutions – that means the ball is in your court."

Okay, I was going to have to communicate on his level if I was going to get through to this guy at all. I needed a game plan. *Think locker room, Dustin. Think ESPN!*

"It was a total accident, sir. A real foul ball. And coming up with a bunch of money isn't exactly going to be – a slam dunk."

For someone who used to think that a quarterback was change from a dollar, I was off to a pretty good start.

Futterman looked peeved. "Well, you or your teacher will just have to think of a way to resolve this situation. That's all there is to it."

The *tap-tap-tap* of his hairy fingers on the desk sounded like a ticking time bomb. Did he think I would come up with something on the spot?

"In our defense, sir, we hardly had any time rehearsing on the set," I finally said. "A rookie mistake. It won't happen next time."

"Next time?" Futterman growled, lunging forward. "There's not gonna be a next time!"

"Why not?"

"Why do you think? It was a disaster!" He pounded on his desk. "I'm just glad no one got seriously hurt. The last thing we need is a lawsuit."

Out of bounds! I'll sell one of Gordy's kidneys or get a job after school declawing cats to pay for the stupid piano. Anything it takes. But there has to be a next time!

"We're ready to step up to the plate now, sir. If you just give us another chance, I know we could really – uh, knock it out of the park."

"You had your chance."

He swings, he misses.

"Oh, and another thing," Futterman said, narrowing his demon eyes.

Now what? I needed a time-out. A seventh-inning stretch.

"That graffiti in the bathroom stall. The cartoon of me in red ink, looking like Frankenstein – I know you did it."

Whoa! That one came out of left field.

"Don't even try to deny it, Grubbs. You were caught red-handed. Literally."

"You're way off base, sir. The graffiti was already there. I was using my red pen to pry open the lock. I fumbled, and it broke."

"Uh-huh. Not to mention lying to me about smoking. You came out of that stall waving a cigar around."

"That was bubblegum! It was purple!"

"Save it, Grubbs," Futterman said, shooting up from his desk. "You're lucky I don't suspend you."

"Kill the ump," I mumbled to myself.

"I'll let the other stuff slide, but as far as the piano is concerned, I'm not letting you out of the dugout. You get me?" He held the door open, waiting for me to leave. "You'd better come up with something – and soon!"

Stee-rike three! And you are outta there!

I walked into the hall and did an actual double take. Jeremy Jason Wilder was sitting on the bench, fidgeting. He couldn't have been in trouble already; there were probably some new-kid forms he had to fill out. Or maybe Futterman wanted his autograph.

"I'll be right with you, Mr. Wilder," Futterman said, and closed his door.

"I heard yelling," Jeremy said.

"Yeah. Don't ask."

"So what's he like?"

"Godzilla on steroids."

Jeremy laughed at that. I was going to just say "see ya" and head home, but something told me to stick around. The blue striped cap that was sitting on his jacket next to him looked familiar.

"Hey, I know that cap," I said.

"You a Yankees fan, Justin?"

"Dustin," I said. "A die-hard fan."

"Really?"

"No! I'm kidding," I said, snorting. *He should only know how much.* "Just a huge fan of *Double Take*. Didn't you wear a cap just like that on the show, when you were Buddy?"

"Yeah, this is it," Jeremy said. He spun the cap on his finger and let it fly off in my direction. "Catch!"

Naturally I missed and had to pick it up off the floor. I'd never laid my hands on real Hollywood memorabilia before.

"Keep it," he said. "It's yours."

"No way! For real?"

"Why not? I have, like, five of them. I walked off with a bunch of cool stuff from the show. Wasn't really supposed to, but, hey – let 'em sue me, right?"

"Right. Thanks!"

I put the cap on – backward, like Buddy used to wear it. I got such a rush, I think I was vibrating.

Futterman poked his head out the door. "Phone call. Just give me five more minutes, okay?" He gave me a strange look before pulling the door shut.

Good. More time for me. After all, it's not every day you hit it off with a TV star. It's not every day a TV star showers you with compliments and presents. *Ask him,* I told myself. *What have you got to lose?*

"So, Jeremy, wanna come to a party?" I blurted out. I was Dustin the Brave. "Just a family thing, but there'll be tons of great food."

"When?"

"The Saturday after spring break. That's, like, in two weeks."

He looked as if he was actually considering it. *I rule!* I did feel a tiny twinge of guilt, though, since I'd already invited Wally. But he never officially RSVP'd about coming, and he kept whining about having to bring a gift. *Hey, when it's someone's birthday, you bring a gift. Get over it.* It'd serve him right if Jeremy said yes.

"Maybe," Jeremy said. "I know it'd make Evelyn happy."

"Really? Who's Evelyn?"

"My mom," Jeremy said. "She wants me to try to fit in around here, make new friends and stuff. I'll let you know on Monday, okay?"

He shoots – he scores!

Chapter 9

You Can Have Your Cake and Edith Too!

The smell of garlic and spaghetti sauce seeped through my bedroom floor and right into my nose. I woke up blinded by the bill of my new Yankees cap, with one cheek covered in drool. I must've been dreaming about Aunt Olive's meatballs. I squinted at the clock. Seven fifty-eight a.m. The troops had probably been up since dawn, cooking for Granny Grubbs's surprise seventy-fifth birthday bash.

Actually, Mom had decided that the "surprise" part of it wouldn't be such a hot idea. "All she needs at her age is a roomful of relatives she hasn't seen in ten years jumping out from behind the furniture and yelling, 'Surprise!'" It was now officially just Granny Grubbs's seventy-fifth birthday bash. I was sprawled out in the hallway painting the new title on a banner when the phone rang.

"Hi, it's me." It was Wally. "I finally came up with a present for your grandma's party. My ma has this shawl she bought in Mexico when she and my dad went on that cruise. Never been worn – it's like brand new. So, what time should I get there tonight?"

Gulp! Jeremy had accepted my invitation almost two weeks before. He was totally cool and had even told me he was "looking forward to the big event" before he disappeared for spring break. Wally hadn't mentioned the party at all since I first brought it up, so I was hoping he'd forgotten all about it. Guess not.

"Hello?" he said.

Just lie, I told myself. *Make it quick and painless.*

"Change of plans, Wal. Party's canceled. Granny's sick."

"Oh. Sorry," he said. "So, wanna take a bus to the mall or something instead?"

"Nah. I'll probably just stay in tonight."

Okay, quick, but not so painless. Lying to your best friend was on par with kicking puppies. I was sure it'd come back to "bite me on the butt" someday, as Granny says. But a guy's gotta do what a guy's gotta do.

Twelve hours later my colorful banner was hanging over the dining-room table downstairs, which was covered in goodies. I had thought we were on a tight budget, but to me it looked like enough food for a sumo-wrestling convention. A roasted turkey was hiding the stain on the fancy lace tablecloth, and surrounding it was a tray of lasagna with meatballs, both potato and macaroni salad, plus three different kinds of cheese – and that was just "the tip of the iceberg lettuce," as Aunt Birdie says. Aunt Olive's masterpiece was hidden on the top shelf in the pantry: a triple-decker chocolate fudge cake with raspberry filling and sprinkles.

Second cousins, great-aunts, and great-uncles arrived one after another, piling their jackets on Aunt Birdie's bed. Mom's boss from the Donut Hole showed up with two boxes of assorted. "Mr. Ortega – Barry – is *my* guest," Mom announced to the family. I wondered if *guest* meant *date*. I could tell from the suspicious looks my aunts gave "Barry" that they were wondering the same thing.

All anyone could talk about (besides "So, who is this Barry Ortega?") was the big television star who was coming. Whenever the doorbell rang, everyone stared at the front door as if the President of the United States were about to walk in. It almost seemed that the party was for Jeremy Jason Wilder and not Granny Grubbs.

"Is that TV boy here yet?" Granny kept asking me.

"Any minute now."

Even she was excited about meeting a sitcom star face to face. I'd never seen Granny so dressed up in my life, and I don't think it was for the sake of Great-Aunt Iris and her husband, Hoyt, from Sheboygan. Her white hair was braided and wound in a bun, like a snake coiled on top of her head. She had on her navy blue church dress – and lipstick! That was a first. Ah, the power of celebrity.

"Maybe you should phone that TV boy's house to see if he's on his way," Granny said. "I'm going to bed soon and I'd sure hate to miss him."

"Bed? But your party barely started!" I said. "There's gonna be cake – and presents."

"I had that mole cluster on my neck removed last week. At my age that's present enough."

"Granny!"

"Well, I'm just saying."

I beelined it to Mom. She'd know what to do.

"We're going to have to do the cake right away," she said, looking worried. "You know your gran – with that arthritis medicine she takes, she can conk out at any minute."

The doorbell rang. Nobody budged.

"That door's not gonna answer itself," Granny said. "It's the TV boy for sure."

I hurried to the front door and stood there with my hand on the doorknob. I couldn't swallow. It felt as if one of Aunt Olive's meatballs were lodged in my throat. I took a second to breathe, then opened the door.

"Hi, Dustin Grubbs!"

It was LMNOP.

"Sorry to interrupt the festivities," LMNOP said in her sloppy lisp, "but I wanted to stop by to wish your grandmother a happy birthday. And give her these."

She pried the lid off the plastic container she was holding. It was loaded with goopy brownies.

"Is that him?" Granny asked. "Where did I put my glasses?"

"No, Gran," I said. "It's just the kid from next door."

The whole room groaned and picked up their dropped conversations and plates.

"He looks different in person," Granny said, squinting out the door. "Kinda girly."

"This isn't Jeremy," I said. "This *is* a girl."

"I'm Ellen, remember? Happy birthday, Mrs. Grubbs," LMNOP said, handing her the brownies. "My mom's gonna need the container back. It's part of a set."

"Well, thank you, sweetheart," Granny said. She picked up the smallest brownie and inspected it closely. "These don't have nuts in them, do they? I'll croak."

"No, ma'am," LMNOP said. "They're nut free." Granny popped the whole brownie into her mouth. "They're chocolate free too. We used organic carob instead."

Granny made a face as if she'd just licked the bottom of a shoe. She spat the brownie into a napkin and handed it to me.

"I don't think that TV boy is coming," she said, half yawning. "I'm going to bed."

"No, Gran, not yet!" I yelled.

There was a knock at the door. I must've slammed it in LMNOP's face without realizing it. She was a pain, but I thought I should at least offer her a cracker or something, so I opened the door.

"Sorry I'm late."

LMNOP was gone, and Jeremy was standing in her place. *He showed!*

My great-aunt's stepdaughter by her second marriage screamed, "It's him!" and dropped a glass.

"That's what I thought too," Granny said, "but it's only the little girl from next door. Don't eat her brownies."

"No, Gran, this *is* Jeremy," I said. "Come on in!"

As soon as he stepped through the doorway, it felt as if everything were going in slow motion, as if this couldn't actually be happening. But there he was, in the flesh, standing in my house with his black leather pants and his shiny black hair.

"Everybody, this is my friend Jeremy Jason Wilder." My stomach jolted when I heard myself say that. "Jeremy, this is everybody."

He'd barely taken off his jacket before he was drowning in a clump of distant relatives.

"Okay, clear the way," Granny said, trotting toward Jeremy. "Don't smother the child before the birthday girl gets a hug."

The lights went out.

"Oh, good Lord," Granny said. "It's happened."

"What's happened?" I asked.

"I've gone completely blind!"

"Happy birthday to you," Aunt Olive warbled.

Everyone gradually joined in the singing and switched attention from Jeremy to Mom, who paraded out of the kitchen carrying the cake. It had a pink 7 candle and a blue 5 candle glowing on top.

Aunt Olive took the last *"to yooou!"* up an octave, drowning out everyone else with her wobbly soprano.

"Give it a rest, Olive," Granny said. "You'll drive all the dogs out of the neighborhood."

Jeremy and I joined the guests gathering around the dining-room table, where Mom placed the cake. Granny hovered over it with her eyelids fluttering, as if she was having a hard time settling on a wish. For a split second the candlelight on her face made her look eighteen.

"Don't tell your wish, Ma," Aunt Birdie said, "or it won't come true."

"Oh, darn it anyway, Birdie! Now I forgot what I was wishing."

"It's okay, Gran," I said. "You'll think of another one."

"I hate to squander the few good wishes I have left. I'm not long for this world, you know."

"Just blow them out already," Aunt Birdie insisted.

"Okay, on the count of three," Mom said. "One . . ." – everyone joined in – "two . . . *three!*"

Granny took another minute. Finally her cheeks puffed out as if she were hitting the high note in a trumpet solo. A gust of air exploded from her that made the Happy Birthday banner flutter and the candle wax splatter. Everyone applauded, and the lights came back on.

Suddenly the cake didn't look so irresistible: sitting in the middle of it, gleaming white against the chocolate frosting, were Granny's false teeth.

"Lost your uppers!" Aunt Birdie said, and snapped a picture.

Granny snatched her teeth and sucked them back into her mouth, like if she did it fast enough, no one would even notice that they had flown out.

Fat chance. The whole room was bent over in hysterics. I thought Jeremy would split his pants from laughing so hard. It wasn't exactly the scene I was hoping for, but at least he looked as if he was having a good time.

Next thing I knew, Great-Aunt Iris asked Aunt Birdie to take a picture of her with Jeremy, and suddenly everyone wanted a picture taken with the big TV star. A line formed.

"Watch the birdie!" Aunt Birdie said, snickering. She was changing positions like a fashion photographer, snapping away so fast, her camera was smoking. "Just strike a pose, say cheese, and keep on moving, people. Ooh, with that swanky red blouse he has on, these'll make stunning Christmas cards!"

I wouldn't have blamed Jeremy if he'd done an about-face and headed for the hills. But he smiled through shot after shot. Finally I grabbed him and led him into the kitchen, where he could have a chance to catch his breath.

"Your family sure is – friendly," he said.

"You mean crazy. You can say it. Sorry they ambushed you like that."

"No prob. I'm used to it," he said, reaching into an open bag of potato chips on the kitchen counter.

"You hungry?" I asked. "All the good food is in the other room, but we could eat it out on the back porch, where it's safe."

He nodded, stuffing his face with chips.

"Okay, I'll go and get it," I told him, heading into the dining room. "Grab us some Cokes from the fridge, and I'll meet you out there."

I was counting on my aunts' cooking to impress Jeremy, 'cause nothing else was going to do the trick. So I piled a little bit of everything onto two paper plates, crammed some napkins into my pants pocket, put two forks in my shirt pocket, and hustled to meet him on the porch.

"Nice breeze," I said, kicking the screen door open. I glided down the stairs, careful not to spill anything, and sat next to Jeremy, who was on the bottom step. "It's like a sauna in that kitchen. Not that I've ever been in one – a sauna, I mean, not a kitchen." *Okay, don't say anything else dumb like that.* I handed him the fuller, neater-looking plate, a napkin, and a fork. "You can have the drumstick if you want," I told him, but he didn't want. "Well, you have to try my aunt's meatballs. You'll die."

"If you say so."

Jeremy stabbed a meatball and shoved the whole thing into his mouth.

"Omigod!"

At least, that's what I think he said.

"Incredible, right?" I said, and stuffed my face with a meatball too. It was burning hot, so I immediately let it drop back onto my plate. "Man, I killed my tongue!"

Jeremy was laughing and speed-chewing at the same time.

"I didn't know those candle-warmer thingies worked so well," I said, wiping sauce off my mouth.

We both took giant gulps of Coke to wash down the meatballs, and without any warning a burp slipped right out of me. Jeremy let one fly too, and we laughed some more. Total connection. I leaned against the railing, gnawing on the turkey drumstick and watching a bug brigade swarm the porch light. Nobody said anything for a while; there was just the sound of distant-distant-relatives chattering and the two of us slurping. But it didn't feel at all uncomfortable.

"You know what?" Jeremy finally said, flicking something off a slice of garlic bread. "I don't think I've ever been to a party like this before."

"A big family get-together?"

"Yeah – well, no. Just a laid-back, come-as-you-are, pick-your-teeth type thing."

Come-as-you-are? Great-Aunt Iris wore a fox stole.

"Or pick-your-teeth-off-the-cake type thing," he said, cracking up. "I thought I'd bust a gut."

"Sorry you had to see that," I said, smiling. "Sometimes my gran forgets to use her denture adhesive."

"Don't worry about it. All old farts start going wacko; they can't help it," he said, scooping up a forkful of potato salad. "But your aunt with the camera – what's her story?"

"Aunt Birdie? What do you mean?"

"She just seems like – I don't know. Is she a little soft in the head or something?"

"Not that I know of."

Another long silence. This one wasn't so comfortable.

"Whatever, I'm cool with it," Jeremy said, chewing. "You should see all the weirdos in L.A."

Anyone else you want to take a stab at while you're at it? Aunt Olive and her off-key singing? Great-Uncle Hoyt and his lazy eye?

"Plastic forks, homemade potato salad – culture shock! This is just a lot different from the Hollywood parties I'm used to," he said, studying my expression. "That's all I was gettin' at."

He should've quit while he was ahead. I stared down at my plate and squashed the yellow guts out of a deviled egg with my fork.

"You mean in a trailer-trashy kind of way, right?"

He didn't say a word after that, and that said it all. The hope that had been building up inside of me – that we'd become friends – suddenly came crashing down. I actually thought I'd heard the *thud,* but it was the screen door's slamming.

"Come on, boys!" Aunt Birdie was bouncing in the doorway in a pointy paper hat, waving us inside. "We're about to do the presents in the living room."

"Hey, I wasn't supposed to bring a present, was I?" Jeremy whispered to me.

"Shucks, no," I said in my best hick voice. I finished the rest of it in my head. *This ain't one of dem fancy-shmancy Hollywood birthday shindigs, where people bring gifts and wear shoes and everythang.*

We left our plates on the porch step and followed Aunt Birdie into the living room. Granny was surrounded by packages and was sitting in the middle of the couch on her "sweet spot" – the sunken-in part where she always sat.

"Well, where've you two been hiding?" Granny said, ripping a sticky-bow off a present and slapping it onto her dress. "I never did get my birthday hug from the TV boy."

She held out her arms and Jeremy was forced into giving her a lingering hug. He drifted to the other side of the room after that, and I plopped down on the couch next to Granny. She had her usual rubbing-alcohol smell, but with the added aroma of old mothballs. *Yep, Jeremy'll be taking that scent home with him as a little souvenir.*

"What am I going to do with another pair of slippers?"

Granny said, tossing aside one of her gifts. "Wool sweaters give me hives." "Never could stand pink." She'd definitely lost the knack of faking delight about a rotten present. But when she opened mine, she snorted and said, "Oh, now that is cute!" It was a T-shirt that read, "I'm not over the hill, I'm still climbing it. That's why I'm so tired all the time." She kissed me on the cheek and held the T-shirt up for everyone to see. Aunt Birdie, who'd been taking flash pictures of Granny opening each gift, went snap-happy.

"Birdie, will you put that darn thing away?" Granny said, pulling a long, flimsy scarf out of a box. "I'm already half-blind in my right eye. Now I'm seeing spots."

"Those are polka dots, Ma," Birdie said. *Snap.* "And you'll thank me later."

"I'll thank you to go throw that thing in the lake!"

"Well, that's everything," Aunt Olive said, gathering Granny's gifts. "You got a lot of nice things, Ma."

"Wait, here's another card, Mother Grubbs," Mr. Ortega said, picking up a pink envelope off the floor and handing it to Granny. "It must've fallen."

Mother Grubbs?

"Oh, that came in the mail for you today," Aunt Birdie said. "No return address."

"Who sent it?" Granny asked, putting on her glasses.

"Open it and see," I said.

Granny tore through the envelope, pulled out the card, and

opened it. She read it to herself, glaring as if it were written in Swahili, then slowly slid it back into the envelope.

"Well, who's it from?" Aunt Birdie asked. "Tammy's House of Beauty?"

"No," Granny mumbled.

"Well, who?" Aunt Olive asked.

"It's from your brother."

"Teddy?" my aunts both said, looking at each other.

That's "Teddy" as in "Theodore," as in "Dad."

My heart just about froze in my chest. Mom's hand flew up to cover her mouth and Aunt Birdie collapsed into a chair. *I thought this wasn't supposed to be a surprise party!* Everyone stopped chattering, stopped chewing, and stared at the card as if it were about to explode.

"You can just throw that in the lake too," Granny said, and flung the card onto the pile of scrunched-up wrapping paper.

The front door flew open and a green-haired Gordy bolted into the room, dragging his new orange-haired girlfriend, Edith. This one came complete with a dog collar, a thorn tattoo, and so many piercings that her head looked like a miniature-golf course.

"Cool," Gordy said, heading for the dining-room table. "There's still cake."

He hacked out a piece of cake and shoved half into his mouth and the other half into Edith's. The whole room cringed.

"What?" Gordy grunted.

That was pretty much the cherry on the trailer-trash sundae. Jeremy was the first to cut out after that. I couldn't resist asking him if he wanted a piece of cake to go. Naturally, he passed. I snuck out of the party early too and went up to bed – funnily enough, before my gran. But not before I could snatch Dad's card out of the garbage pile.

Chapter 10

"It"

"Dustin! Garbage! Now!"

I could tell from Mom's voice that she had finally reached her breaking point. I think that birthday card from Dad really launched her into one of her moods. I could relate. *How come he never sent me a birthday card? Or a letter? A postcard, even?* Maybe he did and it ended up in the trash.

"And I mean now!" Mom yelled.

"Okay, okay."

There was a ton of cleaning up to do the day after the party, but I'd spent most of Sunday in my room, pretending I had a science project I was working on – but really just seeing how long I could lie totally still in bed without thinking a single thought. (Hey, that *is* a science project, kinda-sorta.) Anyway, it was definitely time to get up and face the garbage.

I slid into my flip-flops and plopped my way down the back stairs and into the yard with three bags of trash in tow. The sun was nuzzling the garage and fading fast. And there was a flimsy moon out already, like a smudged, white thumbprint on the turquoise sky. The clanking of the garbage-can lids cut through the quiet in the neighborhood, and I hoped no one would catch me in my cowboys-on-horseback-with-lassos pajamas.

"Hi, neighbor!"

Busted! Of course LMNOP would be in her yard next door. Digging again. Was she searching for dinosaur bones? Tunneling her way out of Buttermilk Falls, maybe? Wishful thinking.

"How'd you like the brownies?" she asked.

Oh, you mean the ones that you probably made out of dirt?

"They were okay."

"Glad ya liked 'em, Dustin Grubbs."

She always called every kid by his or her full name. She didn't get that we were calling her LMNOP – not Ellen Mennopi.

"Cute pj's! I have a pair just like them."

"Cool," I said. "Well, later."

I'm burning these pajamas as soon as I get inside.

"Cinnamon says hi," she lisped.

"Uh-huh. Well, give my regards to your cat."

"We just got this great new kitty litter!" LMNOP said quickly. I was holding the screen door open with my foot, stuck listening to the human mole. "It's biodegradable. Made from all-natural whole-kernel corn."

"I'm happy for you."

"My mom won't let me take Cinnamon outside anymore," she said, screwing the lid on a dirt-filled pickle jar. "Ever since that day you had to rescue her from the roof of our garage. Remember?"

"Yeah. Gotta go."

"I thought you were *great* in the play, by the way. I think you've –"

"Shhh!" I said, pulling the door closed behind me. I sprinted over to the chain-link fence that separated our yards. "My mom doesn't know anything about the play."

"Why not?"

"None of your business."

"Okay, whatever." She brushed her bangs out of her eyes, leaving a track of dirt across her forehead. "I was just gonna say, I think you've got 'it,' Dustin Grubbs," she whispered.

"I do not!" I snapped. "Why? Have you been talking to Nurse Opal? What've you heard?"

"No, no. 'It' – that unexplainable certain something that comes out of you when you're onstage." Her lisp was working overtime. "Not everybody has 'it,' you know."

"And what makes you such an expert? Why do you think I've got 'it'?"

"I can just tell."

"How?"

"Dunno."

I leaned on the fence, waiting for her to say more. She

plucked a plump worm from the ground and watched it wriggle from one hand to the other and then back again. It seemed gigantic in her bony hands. There was skinny, and then there was skeletal, and then there was LMNOP. She probably had to dance around in the shower to get wet.

"So, this 'it' thing," I said, flicking a ladybug off my arm. "What exactly are you seeing?"

"Something jumps out of you, like electricity. It's a gift."

How could someone sprawled out in the dirt, playing worm hockey, be capable of such fascinating conversation?

"Too bad about the play again," she said. "You've had the worst luck. First, with the fire drill, and then the set falling – that's two false starts, and nobody ever got to see the whole play."

"Okay, stop saying *play* so loud, will you? Say – I don't know – say *crab apple* instead."

"Too bad about the crab apple. I can't wait to see it from beginning to end." A smile spread across her face. "So I could really sink my teeth into it."

"Well, that's gonna be a long wait," I said. "Futterman gave it the ax."

"No way!"

"Way. After the piano got wrecked he was fuming. He said he's holding me and Miss Honeywell responsible for the damage – and he's not gonna let us 'out of the dugout' until we raise money for the repairs."

Why was I spilling my guts to LMNOP? I had always thought of her as a kind of nonperson. A nosy little gnat with ice-cube glasses.

"Hmm, I guess that sort of explains the thing with Miss Honeywell," she said, jumping to her feet and disappearing around the garage.

"What thing with Miss Honeywell? LMNOP, get back here and talk to me!"

Did I just say that?

"Nothing, really," she called.

A few seconds later, she rounded the side of the garage, carrying more glass jars and dragging a rusty shovel that was bigger than she was. After leaning the shovel against the fence, she set the jars down carefully and collapsed back into the dirt.

"I saw Mr. Futterman and Mrs. Sternhagen yelling at Miss Honeywell outside of the teachers' lounge the other day," LMNOP said, "and she looked totally stressed out. Did you know stress robs the body of nutrients? It can even make your hair fall out."

"Oh, great!" I yelled, kicking the fence. "Now we'll never get to perform the whole – crab apple. Miss Honeywell was our only hope!"

"Unless . . ."

"There is no unless," I said.

"Unless," she repeated, "you guys can sell tickets and perform it for the general public. That'd raise money."

"Didn't you just hear what I said?" I tapped on my fist as if it were a dead microphone. "Hello? Is this thing on? Futterman said the whole thing was a big mistake. Actually, *fiasco* is the word he used. *Disaster, bomb,* and *nightmare* were some others. He's not going to charge people money to see it. Get real."

"Hmm. What you need is a strategic plan."

"Like?"

"Don't rush me."

LMNOP was tracing circles around the word *It,* which she had written in the dirt with a doll's arm. She looked like a wood nymph casting some sort of spell.

"Maybe . . . maybe if you got your friend Jeremy Jason Wilder to join the cast, then tons of people from miles around would want to come see it. Just like our Buttermilk Falls Pickle Festival – only with a crab apple instead." She looked pleased with herself and tossed the doll's arm over her shoulder and into the empty plastic swimming pool. "Problem solved."

"You've completely lost it! Jeremy's a professional. He'd never sink to being in a stupid school play."

"Crab apple," LMNOP said, springing up. She brushed some dirt off her knees. "Well, you never know till you ask."

"I *do* know. Besides, I think our friendship is pretty much down the toilet."

"Why's that?"

"It just is, okay?"

A loud sigh came from behind the screen door. Aunt Birdie was standing there with a dreamy look on her face, holding a small, fluffy rug.

"It's gonna be good sleeping weather tonight," she said. "Really warm for April."

She stepped into the backyard, letting the screen door slam behind her.

"Well, what have we got here? Romeo and Juliet, spooning under the moonlight?"

"*Ugh!* Aunt Birdie!"

She turned her head and shook the filth out of the rug.

"Oh, I'm just playing with you."

"Gross!" I said. "LMNOP is, like, eight."

"I'm almost ten," she said. "Romeo and Juliet weren't too much older than that, you know."

Just one year younger than me? I thought she was a baby.

"Okay, I'm outta here," I said, 'cause things were getting too creepy.

"Don't go," Aunt Birdie said, coughing from the rug's dust. "I didn't mean to break anything up."

"You didn't," I said. "Believe me."

"But you have to admit, it is the perfect setting. Weeping

willows swaying in a lilac-scented breeze. And the moon is so big, you could take a bite out of it. Like a blessing in the skies."

"Good one!" LMNOP said.

Aunt Birdie gave the rug a big shake and swatted the dust cloud as if it were a swarm of killer bees. Obnoxious kissing noises started coming from the house. When I looked up, I saw Gordy's face pressed into the window screen on the second floor.

"Freakshow and weird girl, sittin' in a tree, k-i-s-s-i-n-g."

"R-e-b-u-l," I shouted.

"You die!" he yelled back, smacking his head on the window frame. Ha!

"You two wait right here," Aunt Birdie said. She was still hacking up a lung. "I'm gonna run inside and get my camera."

"For what?" I asked.

"I want to use up my last roll of film so I can get the party pictures developed," she said, hustling toward the door. "Ellen, wipe that mud off your face and come pose with Dustin in front of our lilac bushes."

"*No!*" I hollered, but my aunt was already inside the house.

I could tell from the expression on LMNOP's face that she liked the idea. No – *loved* the idea. I zoomed past Aunt Birdie and up the hall steps, shot into my room, slammed the door, and took a nosedive under the covers.

Chapter 11

Bankrupt

An hour later, I woke up soaked in sweat. I'd dozed off and dreamt that a baby-grand piano was swallowing me whole. When I stuck my head out from under the covers, I saw my piggy bank sneering down at me from a shelf. There was no use popping its plug. After buying Granny's present and that basketball to bribe Felix into being in the play, I already knew for a fact that it was one hungry pig.

I could try to sell Jeremy Jason Wild-Man's baseball cap on the Internet. I don't really want it anymore. He made it pretty clear that he was slumming it by being at the party – and that he thinks my family belongs in one big padded room.

"You went from hero to zero in my book, buddy," I said, reaching up and ripping the *Double Take* poster off my wall. I wadded it up and flung it at the Yankees-cap shrine on my desk across the room.

That cap would raise some money, but probably not enough to repair a piano. There's no real proof that it was his, anyway. I should've gotten it autographed while I had the chance.

I flopped over on my stomach and started thinking about poor Miss Honeywell, racking her brain trying to think up ways to raise the money – and losing clumps of hair from the stress of it. I wondered if the play was more trouble than it was worth, as Jeremy had turned out to be – and I wondered about my life.

Me, an actor? Yeah, right – when piggy banks fly. I'll probably end up working at the plastics factory when I grow up, just like everybody else in this town.

"Knock, knock, it's your aunt. The pretty one." My bedroom door squeaked open, and Aunt Olive poked her head in. "Are you awake? Can I come in?"

Obviously the *Enter at Your Own Risk!* sign on my door wasn't working.

"So, how's your science project coming along?" she asked.

"Swimmingly."

Her eyes scanned my room, probably searching for Styrofoam planets or papier-mâché volcanoes.

"I'm still in the research stage."

"Okay. Well, I'm off to the grocery store," Aunt Olive said. "I was hoping there'd be some leftovers from the party, but all that's left is the turkey carcass."

"The Grubbses like their grub," I said.

"Can I pick you up anything special?" she asked. "You seem a little down in the dumps."

"No, thanks."

"Are you sure?" Aunt Olive said, putting on her denim jacket with the shiny beads across the top. "I clipped out a coupon for that fishy cereal you like so much. What's it called again?"

"Crustacean Crunch."

"That's it." She started singing in her shaky soprano, "'Crustacean Crunch is fun to munch . . .' How does the jingle go? Sing it with me."

"I don't remember."

I knew what she was doing, but I didn't feel like being cheered up.

"Oh, you know! 'Crustacean Crunch is fun to munch –'"

This could've gone on for days, so I joined in on "'– for breakfast, snacks, and even lunch.'"

Aunt Olive ended on a screechy high note, then launched into something operatic while she checked herself out in the mirror on my closet door. The tip of my jester's belt was sticking out of the closet.

I should hide it in case someone recognizes that it's made out of Dad's old ties – from when he had a real job.

"The curse of working at a bakery," my aunt said, slapping her rear end.

"Aunt Olive, you used to work at Apex Plastics, in Lotus-town, right? Before the bakery? What was that like?"

"It was a paycheck," she said, digging a perfume bottle out of her purse. She gave it two spritzes and twirled into the cloud of perfume. "Why do you ask?"

"That's probably where I'll end up eventually," I muttered. "That's where most people from this town end up."

"Not necessarily."

Aunt Olive dropped the perfume into her purse and scooped out a handful of something crinkly. She sat at the foot of my bed and tossed a rainbow of hard candies across my covers.

"Let me tell you a little story," she said, hunting through the candies. "We Grubbses have greasepaint in our blood. When I was your age, all I ever dreamt about was being on the stage. Sound familiar?" She unwrapped a butterscotch and popped it into her mouth. "Oh, don't look so surprised. You announced it to the world that you want to be an actor."

I socked my mattress and the candies jumped.

"What? How did you –?"

"Gordy told me he saw something on a bulletin board when he picked you up from school."

Motormouth strikes again! That must be the "juicy dirt" he said he had on me.

"Don't worry, I won't blab it to your mom. Anyway, singing is what I really loved. I had a legitimate voice."

Aunt Olive began unbuttoning her jacket as if she was planning on staying awhile. I had a feeling she was about to launch into one of her epic stories that I'd heard a hundred times before.

"So, after high school I auditioned for the Light Opera of Willowbridge, a semiprofessional company a few towns over. I was green, and nervous as a cat. But you know what?"

They cast you in the chorus.

"They cast me in the chorus and made me understudy to Yum-Yum, the ingenue role. It was *The Mikado,* an operetta by Gilbert and Sullivan."

"The Japanese one. I know – I saw the pictures." The part about five curtain calls was just around the corner.

"Two weeks into the run, the woman playing Yum-Yum came down with a bronchial something-or-other, and guess what? I got to go on in her place! Well, long story short –"

Too late.

"– I got five curtain calls that night. Five!" She high-fived the air. "I'll never forget it – the girl playing Peep-Bo tried to convince me to move to New York City with her and audition for the Met." Aunt Olive fiddled with an earring. Her eyes were twinkling. "Wouldn't that have been something?"

That's usually where the story ended. But this time I asked, "Why didn't you?"

"What? Go to New York? Plenty of reasons."

"Like?"

"Well, I met my husband around that time, and he didn't like the whole idea. Things were different back then. After he left me, I moved back into this house, and here I stayed. I still wonder what would've happened in New York." Aunt Olive spat her butterscotch back into its wrapper. "Funny how the sugar-free ones are way too sweet."

I wasn't sure where she was going with this trip down memory lane. *Get to the point!* I thought. I wondered if I'd said it out loud, because the next words out of her mouth were –

"The point is that dreams don't die. They stick with you for the rest of your life. Your dad knew it."

She stopped cold, as if a curse word had accidentally slipped out. It felt as though all the oxygen had been sucked out of the room, just like at the party. That always happened when anyone in the family mentioned my father, which was mostly never.

"Tell me," I said.

"Teddy and I were two peas in a pod when we were young," she said in barely a whisper, glancing toward the open door. "Your dad's a good guy, in spite of everything. Oh, I'm not saying he should win any Father of the Year awards, Lord knows, leaving your poor mom with two boys to raise. That was dead wrong. But he wanted to move to the city more than anything so he could make some sort of living doing what he loved – stand-up. Any city. Your ma wouldn't hear of it."

"I know," I said. "I remember those fights."

"His timing was lousy, but I have to say, he followed his dream."

"Yeah, and deserted us," I grumbled. "Never even bothered to call. If that's what it takes to chase a dream, then forget it."

"Olive, are you still here?" Granny said, appearing in my doorway. I gasped. "I heard your caterwauling from downstairs! Sweet Moses, they could hear it in New Jersey!"

I loved my gran, but she had a habit of butting in at the wrong time. A lot.

"Get the lead out, before the store closes." Granny snapped her dishrag like a lion tamer cracking his whip, then disappeared down the hall.

"*Please* and *thank you* are just not in that woman's vocabulary," Aunt Olive mumbled.

"And don't forget my Earl Grey tea," Granny called. "Decaf!"

Aunt Olive rushed to the doorway and checked to see if the coast was clear. She paused for a second and quietly closed the door.

"Oh, your mom would slap me silly if she knew I was telling you this," she said, sitting beside me on my bed. "Your dad *tried* to stay in touch. After the separation, he called and called."

"No, he didn't."

"Yes. Your mother wouldn't speak to him – she'd just hang

up the phone. Got an unlisted number and everything. Can't say I blame her. She was in a real bad way."

"She still is," I said, "sort of."

"Your gran, too. You saw how she reacted to his birthday card, right?"

I was wondering when that was going to come up.

"How come he never sends me any birthday cards?" I asked.

"He tried." Aunt Olive's voice dropped back down to a whisper and she scooted closer to me. "Just between you, me, and the lamppost, I got a letter from him around Christmastime with his new cell-phone number in it. When I called, he told me he missed you and your brother like crazy, for whatever it's worth. He said he'd sent you kids cards and gifts –"

"We never got anything!"

"Your mom wrote 'Return to sender' on everything – and who knows where they ended up, with him gallivanting all over the country like he does? But he told me he understood, and respected her wishes to cut off all contact. I could tell it was killing him."

I felt like bawling, but I held it in. This was way too much information to absorb all at once. Dad had always been the bad guy in the story; now it was sounding as if Mom was the bad guy.

"Well, where was he when you talked to him?" I managed to squeak out.

"Oh, the Funny Factory or the Giggle Garage or some such place."

"Where?"

"Florida. Boca Raton, I think. That was three or four months ago, but I've spoken to him quite a few times since. He's still got the same cell-phone number." Aunt Olive hooked a fallen wisp of hair behind her ear. "I know he'd love to talk to you."

She stared into my eyes as if she were waiting for an answer to a question that she had never asked. I didn't know what to say. Truth is, everything went numb.

"Oh, for goodness' sake," Aunt Olive said, more to herself than to me. She fished a little book out of her purse, hurried over to my desk, and jotted something down in my spiral notebook.

"Don't tattle on me, Dustin. Promise?" She came over to me, smiling, and waggled my blanket-covered toes. "Or your mother'll have my head on a silver platter."

"Okay."

"Well, I'd better get to the store before that old woman has a conniption."

She gave the top of my head a quick peck and started for the door.

"Aunt Olive," I called, "I'll bet you were an awesome Yum-Yum."

"You know what?" she said, bowing to me Japanese style. "I was."

She left my room with tiny geisha steps, singing,

Three little maids from school are we,
Pert as a school-girl well can be,
Filled to the brim with girlish glee-eee . . .

After hearing the *click* of the door's closing, I threw off the covers, flew over to my desk, and flipped through the spiral notebook until I found the page with the phone number on it. Just staring at those ten digits made my heart gallop. I closed the notebook and shoved it into my backpack, right behind *World History through the Ages*. Dad's birthday card to Granny was hidden between pages 114 and 115. He didn't write anything in it except "Teddy," in black ink. It was a stuffy card with swirly gold writing on the front that said, "Thinking of you, Mother, on Your Special Day," surrounded by roses. I would've expected something a little zippier from a stand-up comic – like bananas in top hats, maybe.

I sat on the edge of my bed, staring into space, trying to remember if I'd ever caught Mom going through my backpack.

The phone rang in the hallway, and I almost hit the ceiling.

"Dustin, it's Pepper again!" Mom yelled.

I made a mad dash to the door.

"Tell her I'll talk to her at school, okay?"

I waited a ten-count for an "okay" back, but it never came.

I bolted the door, then dived halfway under my bed, pulling out suitcases, a tangle of old sneakers, storage bins packed with winter clothes. The red shoe box I was searching for was near the wall, and I managed to kick it out with my foot. I had a sneezing fit from the dust bunnies while I unrolled the rubber bands that kept the lid on. The box had a few old pictures of Dad in it – small ones that used to be in frames. And on the bottom of the box, under some frayed honor-award ribbons, was a silver-star key chain that said *"Reach for the Stars!"* It was the last thing he'd given me before he moved out. On the back was scratched, "To Dusty. Luv, Da." He'd run out of space for the last *d*. Bad planning. Story of his life, I guess.

I lay back on my bed and closed my eyes, clutching that chunk of cold metal. A murky memory started to play out in my head, like an old black-and-white movie.

It's summer, I think. I'm sitting in one of our old vinyl kitchen chairs with my legs dangling. Dad is giving me a haircut and he won't let me look in the mirror until he's all finished. Mom keeps saying, "Don't make it too short, Ted," and telling him to stop getting hairs in her cake batter – or pancake batter; some kind of batter. And we're all sort of singing along with the radio. The Oldies but Moldies station, Dad called it.

Pretty soon the star points started pinching my hand, and I dropped the key chain on the floor.

"Dustin!" Mom called. "Dinner!"

I flung the covers over my head again. I felt hollow inside – like that ugly ceramic pig on my shelf.

Chapter 12

Catching the Worm

I headed to school extra early the next day so I could grab Miss Honeywell as soon as she showed up. (Well, not really "grab.") We had to come up with a brilliant money-raising scheme to get the piano repaired if we wanted half a chance of getting the play up and running again. Futterman was still dead set against it, but maybe Miss Honeywell could work her magic on him if that dented piano weren't standing in her way.

The playground was totally empty. Quiet too, except for the cheeping birds and my chattering teeth. It was chilly out, and little cloud puffs were coming out of my nostrils. *I hope Futterman doesn't see me – I might get accused of smoking again.* I sat on a swing with a direct view of the teachers' parking lot, waiting for Miss Honeywell's light blue convertible to pull in. So far only the sheriff's car had driven by. Twice.

"Hey, early bird!" Pepper yelled, waving to me from the

sidewalk, where she was surrounded by an audience of squirrels. She rounded the fence and ran over to me, chomping on a drippy breakfast burrito. "Jeez, squirrels'll eat anything. What're you doing here at this ungodly hour?"

"I need to talk to Miss Honeywell about the stupid piano," I said, yawning. "What's your excuse?"

"My stepdad dropped me off, like, ten minutes ago – he has to do inventory at the factory. I don't even think they unlock the school's main doors till around eight, do they?"

"Probably not," I said, checking my watch.

Pepper hopped up onto the swing next to me. "Oh, gawd!" she yelped. "These are all dewy. Our butt cheeks are gonna have rings on them."

"We'll live," I said. I pushed off from the ground to start the swing going. "So why were you calling me last night?"

"Oh, right – and thanks for *not* getting back to me. I just wanted to warn you, that's all," she said, shoving the last of the burrito into her mouth. "Wally's on the warpath."

"Uh-oh. Tell me."

"He's not speaking to you."

I swung higher, afraid to ask for the grimy details. Pepper finished swallowing her food and tossed the burrito wrapper into a nearby trash can. A perfect shot.

"Why not?" I finally asked.

"He told me that you flat-out lied to him about your grandmother's party being canceled."

I dug my heels into the dirt to stop the swing and nearly fell off.

"I guess his mother was driving by your house and saw a bunch of cars parked in front," she said, turning around and around in her swing so that the chains twisted. "Wally took his bike over to your house to check it out. I think he said he saw you and Jeremy sitting on the back porch or something."

"Oh, man," I said.

"Is that true?" Pepper said, still turning and twisting. "Did you lie?"

I didn't answer.

She lifted both feet off the ground and spun like a tornado, with the swing chains jangling. Her short red hair stood straight out, then fell flat again when she came to a stop.

"'Cause that's a slimy thing to do if it's true," she said, jumping off the swing and grabbing onto a pole. "Oh, I think I'm gonna puke."

"Miss Pew! Mr. Grubbs!"

It was Mrs. Sternhagen, calling from the parking lot. I guess we must've missed her flying in on her broomstick.

"Speaking of puke," I said.

"I need your assistance, please," Mrs. Sternhagen said, snapping her fingers.

I knew it. As soon as Pepper and I got to the parking lot, Mrs. Sternhagen handed us two shopping bags each. One of mine was filled with boxes of macaroni and glue, so either she'd be making a mighty nasty lunch, or her second-graders would be making some mighty ugly pencil holders.

"I understand Principal Futterman had a word with you about the piano in the auditorium, Mr. Grubbs," she said, leading us toward the school's side entrance. "And that nothing has come of it."

"Yes, ma'am – or no, ma'am."

"And your teacher apparently doesn't feel it's her responsibility. I've been heartsick ever since that play of yours, when the accident happened." She stopped and looked directly at me. "My family donated that piano to Buttermilk Falls Elementary. It belonged to my grandfather at one time."

"Oh," I said. "I didn't know that."

"It's such a lovely instrument," Pepper said, rolling her eyes in my direction.

"And graduation is not too far away." Her high heels were clacking again. "I don't know how we're going to have a proper graduation without me at the keyboard, playing the traditional *Pomp and Circumstance*."

That would be the end of civilization as we know it.

She kept on yammering as we walked up the stone steps and through the teachers' entrance at the side of the school. On our way to her classroom, I spotted two heads bobbing around the desk in Nurse Opal's office. One was golden blond with loose, bouncy curls. It definitely belonged to Miss Honeywell. She must've parked on the street for some reason, 'cause her car wasn't in the lot. And the other head belonged to – Jeremy? I wasn't 100 percent sure.

After we dropped off the shopping bags (without so much as a thank-you – or a tip), Mrs. Sternhagen recruited Pepper into helping her shelve a stack of easy readers. I escaped with a story about having carpal tunnel syndrome and sped back to the nurse's office to peek through the glass in the door.

It *was* Jeremy. He was squirming behind an open textbook. There was oral reading. Nodding. More reading. It looked as though some sort of private lesson was going on.

"Spying, Mr. Grubbs?" Futterman barked.

I hate it when people sneak up on you like that.

"Just wondering if the nurse is here yet," I lied – again. I think I was becoming addicted. "Pepper said she was gonna puke."

That part was true, but she didn't really mean it, I don't think. "The truth cleverly told is the biggest lie of all." That's what Granny says. What was happening to me?

"Do yourself a favor and put your energies into something useful," Futterman said, steering me away from the door with a firm hand on my shoulder. "Like coming up with a way to raise funds for the piano, perhaps?"

He was wearing me down to the nub with this piano thing.

"Funny you should mention that, 'cause that's why I'm here so early – to talk to Miss Honeywell about it."

"Miss Honeywell's 'well' seems to have run dry on the subject." His fat face said that he was proud of that little "un-pun." "I want to know what you've come up with."

"Uh, I don't know. A PTA bake sale? Candy drive? Car wash? Bike-a-thon?"

"Nickels and dimes, Mr. Grubbs," he said. "You can do better than that. You're supposed to be a creative kid – so create!"

Out of desperation I mentioned LMNOP's stupid suggestion: Jeremy + Play = $$$. Futterman didn't answer. But I swear I saw dollar signs *ka-ching* in his eyeballs.

First thing Tuesday morning, after the usual buzzing and burping of our classroom loudspeaker before daily announcements, our beloved principal's voice came bellowing through.

"Good morning, students! This is Principal Futterman. Judith, is this working? I just hear crackling. Testing, testing. Batter up, batter up. Okay. And can you get me some strong black coffee? Good morning, students."

It was usually our vice principal's voice that we heard, announcing crossing-guard schedules, menu changes in the cafeteria – that sort of thing. Futterman rarely came on unless he had something important to say. My class stopped blabbing and actually paid attention when they heard that it was the head honcho.

"Just a few quick announcements," he said. "Number one: the National Science Fair applications have to be turned in no later than noon tomorrow – and I'd like to see Buttermilk

Falls well represented this year. We haven't had any entrants since Andrew Glickman blew the competition away two years ago with his wind generator."

He laughed at his lame joke.

"So I strongly urge all you budding scientists to participate. (*Throat-clearing.*) Item number B: The gym floor is being revarnished, starting today. Nobody'll be allowed near the gymnasium for a solid week."

I silently cheered against the class's groans.

"But gym classes will still be held at their usual times, on the playground."

I silently groaned against the class's cheers.

"Just put it right there, Judith, thanks. I really need it this morning. And I could use some sugar too. More. More. (*Slurp.*) Oooh, hot, hot, hot!"

Even Miss Honeywell cracked up at that.

"And last, but not least, there will be a meeting of the sixth-grade cast and crew of *The Crook in the Crowded Castle*. Huh? Oh. *The Castle of the Rookie Clowns – Crooked* – uh, the play. It'll be held in the auditorium this Thursday at three-thirty sharp. Be on time. That's it. Have a productive day! Judith, how do you turn this –?" *Buzz. Crackle. Click.*

Chapter 13

Peeling the Onion

The cast and crew (stinky Leonard Shempski) of *The Castle of the Crooked Crowns* filed into the first two rows of the auditorium. Wally was doing his thing where he pretends I don't even exist. He sat as far away from me as possible. Sitting on the edge of the stage, next to the tarp-covered piano, was a large, round woman wearing a scarf headband, a black sweat suit, and pink ballet slippers.

"Welcome, kiddles!" she bellowed. "For those of you who don't know me, I'm Miss Regina Van Rye. I've been the kindergarten teacher here for the last year."

She talked really loud and was shaped just like the piano. I couldn't believe I'd never noticed her before. You'd think she'd be hard to miss.

"Now, let's put on our quiet faces and settle down."

I'd been psyched ever since Futterman's announcement.

This meeting was definitely a good sign – still, nobody knew for sure what it was really about.

"Why are you smiling, doofus?" Darlene hissed, elbowing me. "I bet they make us all pitch in to pay for the stupid piano!"

"I know you're all curious as kittens, so let's dive in head-first," Miss Van Rye said. *"The Castle of the Crooked Crowns* is up and running again! Hallelujah!"

"Woo-hoo!" I howled. Confetti shot out of a tiny cannon in my head.

"Principal Futterman has decided to present it to the general public as a school fund-raiser," she continued, "for one performance only. And since he'll be charging 'dough-re-mi' for the tickets, he thinks the play could use a little tweaking. Enter *moi!*" Miss Van Rye's arm flew over her head and she posed like a Spanish dancer. "I will serve as your new director!"

"What happened to Miss Honeywell?" I asked.

"Well, uh – Principal Futterman thought your teacher had too much on her plate right now to take on this project."

What a crock! It was her project to begin with.

"This is going to be thrilling, tadpoles," Miss Van Rye said. "The roar of the greasepaint, the smell of the crowd!"

All I smelled was a rat. And Leonard Shempski. Well, at least the play was on its feet again – and with a real audience, coughing up the bucks.

"Of course, I'll understand if anyone wants to drop out of

the play for any reason," Miss Van Rye said. "But let me know ASAP, so I have time to replace you."

Darlene Deluca and Millicent Fleener both raised their hands.

"Oh, before I forget, there's already been one small cast change," Miss Van Rye said, scanning the seats. "Hmm, I don't see him."

Just then Jeremy Jason Wilder pushed through the auditorium doors. I gasped, along with everyone else.

"Speaking of the devil," Miss Van Rye said. "Right on cue!"

"Sorry I'm late," Jeremy mumbled.

"What's he doing here?" Pepper whispered to me.

LMNOP's harebrained idea must've worked!

"Jeremy will be replacing Felix Plunket as the Prince," Miss Van Rye said. "Much to the relief of Felix, by the way."

The cast applauded while Jeremy collapsed into an empty seat. He looked about as thrilled as a criminal just sentenced to five hundred hours of community service.

"Welcome, Jeremy!" Miss Van Rye said. "You'll definitely add some real star power to our production."

Now I hated her. *The Prince isn't the star; the Jester is the star. Did she even read the script?*

"So who were the young ladies who had their hands up?" Miss Van Rye asked.

"Never mind," Darlene and Millicent said, eyeballing Jeremy as if he were dipped in chocolate.

"Good answer. Okay, just so you don't think Principal Futterman has completely lost his marbles by putting the kindergarten teacher in charge of the production, I'll fill you in on a little of my background in the theater."

Miss Van Rye dug into her giant straw tote bag and pulled out what looked like an old scrapbook.

"Now, I'm not one to toot my own horn – oh, who am I kidding?" She laughed a musical laugh that covered a full octave. "But seriously, kiddles, after college I studied acting at the renowned Actor's Loft, in New York. That was followed by two straight seasons at the Harmonies 'n' Hash Dinner Theatre in Pittsburgh, where I got stellar reviews," she said, hugging the scrapbook. "If anyone's interested, I made copies."

I sort of liked her again. She reminded me of my aunt Olive – times ten. I glanced at Jeremy to see if he looked impressed and caught the tail end of an eye-roll. It was obvious that he didn't want to be there, and I wondered why he was. Futterman must've scared him into it somehow.

"Okay, fellow thespians, put your scripts away. You're not going to need them just yet," Miss Van Rye said, rolling onto her feet. "Everybody onstage for some warm-up exercises. Come on, up, up, up! Quick like bunnies!"

On our way up to the stage, I heard Wally ask Pepper, "What's a thespian?"

She shrugged.

"Another word for *actor*," I said, without looking directly at him. He pretended not to hear me, record-breaking grudge holder that he was. I guess I deserved it, though.

The cast spread out, taking up the whole stage. Wally went somewhere stage left. A bunch of girls were racing for a spot near Jeremy and ended up shoving me right next to him.

"Hey," Jeremy said to me.

"Hey," I echoed.

It felt uncomfortable – just like that first conversation we'd had in the cafeteria.

"All righty, let's begin by warming up our mouths," Miss Van Rye said. "Really work 'em." She paraded in front of us, distorting her face and flopping her tongue way out like a dog chewing gum. "Mwah, mwaaah, blaaah, bloooy, yah-yah-yah!" Little by little we followed her lead. The thought crossed my mind that she might've been putting us on and she'd have a good yuck about this when she got home, but I decided I was wrong.

"Now repeat what I say," she said. "The lips, the teeth, the tip of the tongue."

A tongue twister. My favorite! We repeated it, getting faster and faster, like a speeding train; then Miss Van Rye held up her hands to stop a train wreck from happening. She reached into her tote bag, removed a plastic container, and handed it to Jeremy.

"Here, take one and pass around the rest," she said. "One to a customer."

I didn't have a clue what was in the container until Jeremy passed it to me. Wine-bottle corks? *I wonder if she polished off a crate of wine last night, just so we'd have enough.*

"Okay, all eyes on me," Miss Van Rye said. "Oh, I just love it when all eyes are on me! Now take your cork and place it between your front teeth, like so." She bit the cork, and her hand circled beneath her chin. "The lips. The teeth. The tip of the tongue."

"Excuse me, Miss Van Rye," Darlene said, "but why does Leonard have a cork? He's crew. Should the crew have a cork?"

She ignored Darlene and started us on our next tongue twister, "Unique New York." It sounded more like "Ooohneee noo yor," and we all had long strings of spittle dangling from our chins.

"No, no, no," Miss Van Rye said, removing the sloppy cork from her mouth. "You're dropping the last consonant. It's 'New York-k-k'! Try it again, and I want you to splatter the back wall of the auditorium with *k*'s."

"This is too hard," Darlene said, massaging her jaw. "And icky."

"It ensures proper enunciation," Miss Van Rye said. "It just takes practice."

"But it hurts!"

"Show business isn't for wimps, dear. You have to suffer for your art."

"When are we gonna get to the play?" Darlene whined. "I'm getting lockjaw!"

"Oh, stick a cork in it," Miss Van Rye said, giggling at her own joke.

Wally snorted and the cork shot out of his mouth, whacking Darlene above her ponytail. She screamed so loud, you'd think somebody had slammed a piano lid on her knuckles.

"Idiot!" she yelled. "You did that on purpose!"

"Did not!" Wally said, laughing. "I swear."

"It was a total accident," I said, laughing too. "I saw the whole thing."

"It's not funny!" Darlene said, holding up a fist. "He could've knocked an eye out!"

"Just the one in the back of your head!" Wally said.

"Kiddles, kiddles!" Miss Van Rye clapped her hands. "Save these raw emotions for your performances. Maybe we've done enough tongue twisters for today."

Ya think? My tongue was in knots, and the stage looked like swampland.

"In fact, why don't we take a well-earned potty break? Ten minutes, everyone."

"Potty break"? You can take the actress out of the kindergarten teacher, but you can't take the kindergarten teacher out of the actress.

Wally walked right past me and out into the hall, even

though I'd just stuck up for him. That's gratitude for you. I noticed Miss Van Rye take a Jack Sprat Donuts bag out of her tote and inhale two French crullers. I wondered if she'd run into Mom at the Donut Hole – she'd better not have spilled the beans about my being in the play.

A loud squeak came from the back of the house. Jeremy was sitting in the last row, wearing headphones. We'd barely said a word to each other since the party, so I didn't know what his deal was. I was dying to know how Futterman had worked his evil genius and persuaded him to be in the play. *There's no law against acting friendly, even if you're not feeling friendly – after all, acting is what I do. Plus, the Prince and the Jester have three scenes together. I don't want any tension between us mucking up my performance.* I took the long way around the auditorium and sat one seat away from him. He was listening to a CD and staring at the cover of *Celeb* magazine. "The Fifty Sexiest Celebrity Belly Buttons" was splashed across the top.

"How do you do a cover story on belly buttons?" I asked. "Do they, like, divide them into innies and outies? Fuzzy and bald? Pierced and bejeweled?"

Nothing. Maybe he didn't hear me. Or maybe he didn't feel like slumming it at the moment.

"You can have your Yankees cap back if you want," I said.

Still nothing. I repeated it with more oomph.

"Huh?" He took off his headphones. "Why would I want it back?"

"Dunno."

Jeremy put his feet up on the armrest in front of him and started thumbing through the magazine.

"Nice shoes," I said.

"Yeah, they're the new Bruno Vitale suede loafers. Three hundred bucks."

All the clothes in my closet weren't worth three hundred bucks.

"Cool," I said.

I could tell he wasn't in a talky mood, but at least he was saying something.

"I'm sort of surprised you're doing the play," I said, getting right to the point. "I mean, you being you and all. Oh, I'm glad you are, though. Really, really glad."

"Really, really glad"? I can't believe what passes through these lips sometimes.

Long silence. I was losing him. I had to change the subject – *stat!*

"So, celebrity belly buttons?" I said, pretending to be interested.

"Yep."

"What does it say in the small print under 'Navel Academy Awards'?" I asked, leaning in. Jeremy gave me one of those annoyed sighs, as if I'd asked him to sort fish heads or something. But he picked up the magazine and began reading out loud.

"'East Coast or West, casual or glam, the beee –'" He stopped. Blinked. "'Casual or glam, the –'" He tossed me the magazine. "Here, you read it."

"'The beguiling belly button is back.' I didn't know it was missing."

Jeremy ripped the magazine out of my hand and put his headphones back on. Conversation over.

What did I say? What did I do? Now who was acting psycho? To quote Aunt Birdie, "That was the straw that broke the cannibal's back." Suddenly I wanted to knock those headphones off his inflated head and shake him. *I invited you into my home, dude! I lost my best friend because of it, Mr. Hollywood hotshot!* I made a mental note to beat up his baseball cap the minute I got home.

After the break we still didn't take out our scripts. We did what Miss Van Rye called the mirror exercise. She had us sit face to face with different partners, copying each other's exact movements in slow motion. Jeremy got stuck with Darlene first. I could see her making pucker lips an inch from his face. He looked as if he were being tortured, but he was forced to make the same lovey-dovey faces right back at Darlene. *Ha!*

When it came around to Wally and me as partners, we

could barely even look at each other. It was intense. I thought I might break through his wall of hate by making blowfish cheeks and pig snouts. But no such luck.

"Oh, I can't believe it's six o'clock already!" Miss Van Rye said. "Tonight I want you all to think about what makes your characters tick. Find the different layers. Peel the onion."

"I don't get it, Miss Van Rye," Wally said. "Why do we have to peel onions?"

"That's just a figure of speech," she explained. "I want you to dig beneath the surface of your characters. Really delve."

"Oh, man, that sounds like homework!" Wally complained.

"Yeah," Darlene said. "I wouldn't mind delving if I was playing Princess Precious – the role I was born to play."

"La-la-la-la-la." Miss Van Rye stuck her fingers in her ears. "Fiddle-dee-dee, fiddle-dee-dee!"

I chimed in with "I think this is great, Miss Van Rye. What kinds of things are we looking for?"

"Now you're talking! For example, what are your character's hopes and dreams, likes and dislikes? Down to the smallest details, such as, What does he eat for breakfast?"

"Or if he's an innie or an outie," I said.

"Exactly!"

I glanced at Jeremy. My brilliant belly-button reference went unnoticed.

Millicent Fleener stopped scribbling in her notepad and raised her hand.

"Yes, Millicent?"

"I only have two lines. Do I still have to delve?"

"It couldn't hurt," Miss Van Rye said. "Remember, there are no small parts, only small actors."

"Yes, ma'am." Millicent looked disappointed.

"Well, nice work today, munchkins," Miss Van Rye said, applauding us. "Bravo!"

Jeremy grabbed his stuff and shot out the door like a bullet.

"Oh, one more thing, cast!" Miss Van Rye said. She was wedged in a front-row seat, struggling out of her ballet slippers. "There are show posters in the cardboard box stage right – hot off the presses. Principal Futterman is really going all out. Everyone take a stack before you leave. I expect to see Buttermilk Falls plastered in these things."

"Oh, man," Wally grumbled.

"Get some rest, boys and girls. Tomorrow we begin reblocking the show."

"What the heck's 'blocking'?" I heard Wally ask Cynthia.

"Where you move to onstage," I said.

He stomped away from me and stood in line at the box of posters. Pepper and I followed and ended up holding our breath behind Leonard Shempski.

"Jeez," Pepper said. "How are we supposed to delve, plaster, *and* get some rest?"

"Well, munchkin," I said in my best Miss Van Rye voice, "show business isn't for wimps. You have to suffer for your art!"

Wally gave me a quick look over his shoulder.

"Knock it off," Pepper said, snickering. "You're gonna get us in trouble."

"Fiddle-dee-dee! Fiddle-dee-dee!" I said, sticking my fingers in my ears.

The old Wally would've been howling at that, but he just grabbed some posters and left. We'd had rough patches in our friendship before, but this time I think I screwed things up big time.

Chapter 14

Yankee Doodle Dilemma

"Can I help you, young man?"

The waitress from the Yankee Doodle Diner had a tower of blond hair with an old army hat angled on top.

"Yes, ma'am," I said. "We're doing a play down at the school. Is it okay if I put this poster in your window?"

"We've already got one in the entranceway. Didn't you see it on your way in?"

"Oh, sorry, I –"

"One more's not gonna hurt, I guess," she said. "Why don't you go ahead and take out the one from St. Agatha's pancake breakfast? That was last year, for heaven's sake."

"Thanks," I said. I took the faded poster out of the window, shook off the dead flies, and handed it to the waitress, Bunny. Her name tag stood out against the stars-and-stripes handkerchief that was pinned to her pocket.

I hadn't been to the diner in months, but it looked different, as if Uncle Sam had exploded in there or something. Tiny American flags were poking out of everything.

"I like how you fixed up the place," I said.

"Well, ever since that Jukebox Café opened across the street, we started losing business," Bunny said. "So Ed and I are pulling out all the stops. This place is our dream, and we'd sure hate to lose it."

"I know what you mean," I said.

It looked as if sticking a feather in its cap wasn't doing the Yankee Doodle Diner much good, though. Besides the dead flies, there were just a few people at the counter and old Mr. Kravitz, the pharmacist, sitting in one of the booths, sipping an iced tea.

"Oh, miss? Miss?"

The voice coming from behind the menu at the counter sounded real familiar.

"I'd better get back to my customers," Bunny said, trotting away.

"Can I have that order of fries *to go,* instead of for here?"

It was Wally, using a deeper voice, as if I wasn't going to recognize him. It was the same exact voice he used as the King. He turned his back to me, facing the revolving dessert case.

"The Star-Spangled Banana Cream Pie came in fresh today," Bunny said, tapping her order pad with a pencil. "Can I tempt ya?"

"Nah, I'm not a big fan," Wally said.

"Those Red-White-and-Blueberry Muffins are to die for. No? How about your friend?" she asked, looking my way. I was lingering near the gum-ball machine at the entrance.

"Him?" Wally said. "He's not my friend. And can you hurry with my fries, please?"

"Well, you boys both came in with the same posters, so I just figured –"

"Nothing for me, thanks," I said.

Bunny stabbed her pencil into her lacquered hair and yelled, "Okay, Ed, put some wheels on those frog sticks!"

"Remind me what that means again," the cook said from the kitchen area.

"Make the fries to go! For Pete's sake, get with the program."

I knew Wally wasn't going to run away as long as he had food coming. I wandered toward him, wondering what was going to come out of my mouth. *Why is some stuff, like "I'm sorry," practically impossible to say?*

"So I guess you hate my guts, right?" I said, approaching him.

Wally plunked his clunky bassoon case on the stool next to him, forming a barrier between us. I sat on the next stool over.

"Listen, Wally –"

"It's Wallace."

"Pepper filled me in on what happened," I said. "About you seeing Jeremy at my house and everything. Would it help if I said . . . that it was a huge mistake?"

"No."

This was going to take a while. I grabbed a handful of Sweet 'n' Slim packets out of the small bowl on the counter and piled them in front of me.

"It definitely should've been *you* at that party instead," I said.

"You must be confusing me with somebody who cares," Wally snapped, burying his head in the menu again.

He wasn't making this any easier.

"Sorry I lied. For whatever it's worth."

There. I'd actually said the word *sorry,* but Wally couldn't care less. I focused my attention on balancing four Sweet 'n' Slim packets on their edges to build the foundation of a fort.

"But you were complaining about having to get my gran a gift," I went on, "and then I never heard back from you, so –"

"So you just blew me off," Wally snapped, spinning around on his stool to face me.

"Hey, you never officially RSVP'd! That doesn't count as a blow-off."

The bells on the door jingled, but I was too busy with my fort to turn around and see who'd come in.

"Oh, hi, Dustin Grubbs. Hi, Wallace Dorkin."

"Hi, LMNOP," Wally said. "See, at least *she* calls me by my right name."

My annoying neighbor dropped some coins in the Paws Across America pet-adoption canister next to the cash register and came bouncing over to us.

"I just ran into Pepper Pew, and she told me the play is on again!" she said. "Are you guys psyched? Are these the posters? Spectacular!"

Her lisp shot spittle clear across the room.

"Say it, don't spray it!" I said.

"Sorry. I could take a bunch and post them around town, if you want."

"Sure. Knock yourself out."

LMNOP grabbed some posters and struggled to fit them under her scrawny arm.

"So, I hear Jeremy Jason Wilder's gonna be in it," she said.

Wally slammed the menu down.

"Yep," I said.

She probably wants my undying gratitude for taking her up on her suggestion.

"I have to talk to you," she said in my face. "It's important."

"We're kind of in the middle of something," I said.

"But I think you're really going to want to –"

"Later, okay?"

LMNOP swung her backpack over her shoulder, nearly toppling to one side, and stood there, staring. I wasn't sure which thing grossed me out more – her muddy fingernails or the *I'm Terrific!* pin on her backpack.

"All righty, then," she said, finally heading out. "Bye, Wallace Dorkin. Bye, Dustin Grubbs."

I went back to building my fort.

"That girl is just so sweet," Bunny said, bringing Wally his greasy bag of fries. "Comes in here every other day to give money for the homeless animals. Ain't that something?" She slapped the check onto the counter.

"Skinny little thing," Mr. Kravitz said, chuckling. "I thought she was a crack in the wall."

"Oh, Frank, stop!" Bunny said, flipping through her order pad.

"She said 'Grubbs,' didn't she?" Mr. Kravitz said, shaking a crooked finger at me. "Are you Ted Grubbs's boy?"

My Sweet 'n' Slim fort collapsed.

"Guilty," I said.

"I remember when you were knee high to a grasshopper. Nice man, your father – always with the jokes," Mr. Kravitz said, standing up. He tucked a dollar under his empty glass. "Used to bring you and your brother into my drugstore on Sundays for root-beer floats way back when I still had the soda fountain."

I could barely remember stuff like that.

"Give my regards to your pop, son," Mr. Kravitz said, drifting toward the exit. "And tell him to be sure and stop by the store real soon."

"Don't hold your breath," I mumbled.

"How's that?"

"You bet."

"Miss?" Wally said. "Do you think I can get some water to go too? With lots of ice? There's no charge for that, is there?"

"It's on the house," Bunny said, raising a painted-on eyebrow. "Adam's ale, extra hail!" she called out on her way to the ringing phone.

I started again from scratch with Fort Sweet 'n' Slim. Wally looked over the check and took his wallet out of his backpack. Well, he called it a wallet, but it was really a change purse.

"Oh, crud!" he said, looking inside it. He zipped it, unzipped it, then zipped it again. "I totally can't believe it!" He searched through all his pockets, then his backpack. More pockets.

"Okay, Ed," Bunny yelled, hanging up the phone. "Burn one, take it through the garden, and pin a rose on it!"

"Come again?" the cook said.

"Hamburger with lettuce, tomato, and onion!" Bunny said, storming into the kitchen. "How many times do we have to go over this?"

"Wouldn't it be easier to just say 'hamburger with lettuce, tomato, and onion'?" I asked, turning to Wally – but he wasn't there. I heard rattling. The Walrus was by the cash register, trying to shake coins out of the Paws Across America can. I slid down off my stool and hurried over to him.

"You can't do that!" I whispered. "It's illegal."

"Not if I put the money back tomorrow," he said, plucking

a nickel from the slot in the canister. "Besides, it's none of your business."

I looked to see if anyone was watching us. There was only one man at the counter now, and he was buried in a newspaper. Black smoke that smelled like deep-fried sneakers was seeping out of the kitchen, and Bunny was waving a rag around, chewing out the cook.

"Jeez, Wal," I whispered, "I can't believe you're so pigheaded that you'd rather commit a crime than ask a friend for help."

"Okay, then," he said, slamming down the can. "Can I borrow fifty cents?"

I checked my jacket pockets and pulled out some loose change.

"All I have are a few pennies and that Canadian nickel from when those jerks threw them at us during the play," I said, and handed him the coins. "Otherwise I'm bankrupt."

"Some help."

Wally rattled the canister again and three dimes fell out.

"Jackpot!" he said, scooping them up. "Okay, now I've got exactly enough. But no tip."

"Here comes the waitress!" I warned. "I think maybe she saw."

Bunny poured a coffee refill for the man at the counter, then swung behind the cash register with Wally's cup of ice water and a straw.

"You ready?" she said, giving us a suspicious look.

Wally paid his bill mostly in pennies. Bunny counted the change out loud, moaning every ten cents or so. She shoved the register door closed with her hip and gave us a limp salute. "Have a Yankee Doodle day, now."

Wally and I grabbed our stuff with Bunny staring us down. We were almost out the door when she called, "I wish you boys all the luck in the world with that play of yours!"

We hit the sidewalk running and didn't stop until we got to Main Street.

"I don't think she really meant it when she said to have a Yankee Doodle day, do you?" I asked Wally, catching my breath.

"Why? She wished us luck with the play, didn't she?"

"Yeah, but there are *two* kinds of luck. Think about it. Good luck and . . ."

Even with the clue, it took a while before Wally's face registered that he got it.

We headed down Main with Wally walking a few feet away from me. That meant he was still mad, but things were definitely moving in the right direction. I tried to stay in rhythm with the *thwack-thwack-thwack*ing of Wally's bassoon case as it hit his leg. By the time we reached Cubberly Place, we were walking side by side. I think we'd automatically slipped back into being full-fledged best friends.

"Watch this," Wally said with a bunch of fries sticking out

of his mouth. "The lips, the teeth, the tip of the tongue. The lips, the teeth, the –"

"Knock it off," I said. "We're in public."

"Fry?"

"No, I'm good."

That felt like a normal moment. I was out of the woods.

"Wow, look at that sky," I said.

Fiery orange and pink streaks were melting into the horizon ahead of us. Wally and I were practically melting too. It was unusually hot out, considering it was barely spring – and even though the sun was setting, it was still packing a punch. We stopped to put up a poster on the bulletin board in the Laundromat. It was boiling in there, but at least it smelled like clean sheets. That's when Wally saw the flyer.

"Oh, look! My bassoon teacher said he could get me two free tickets to this," he said, all excited. "I almost forgot. He's performing with the Verdant Valley Chamber Ensemble at the high school Saturday night. Wanna come?"

I knew I should've jumped at the chance, just to get on his good side. But classical music gave me a stomachache. I'd rather listen to alley cats in heat.

"Can't you take your mom?"

"Come on, man, you owe me big time," Wally said. "And they're doing a piece featuring bassoon. Nobody ever does a piece featuring bassoon."

"Maybe there's a reason for that," I mumbled.

"Huh?"

"Nothing."

After we left the Laundromat, we took our usual route home. Except for the sound of Wally chomping on ice cubes, we passed by four antique stores in complete silence. The distance between us was widening again. We got to the end of the block, stepped off the curb, and then –

"Selfish."

"What?" I said. I smelled another fight brewing – and after we'd barely made up.

"You can really be selfish sometimes," Wally said.

"Just because I can't go to the stupid concert with you makes me selfish?"

"Won't – not can't – it's not stupid – and yes."

"How?"

"I did you a favor by being in your *stupid* play, and you can't do me a favor by – oh, forget it."

We stopped when we got to the other side of the street. Wally crushed the empty bag and paper cup and lined them into a garbage can.

"Favor? You have a great part," I said, digging a roll of tape out of my backpack. "The King is a great part!"

"Oh, who cares? I only agreed to do the play in the first place 'cause you're my best friend. It's turning out to be a real pain."

"How can you say that?"

I ripped off four pieces of tape with my teeth and stuck them to the corners of a poster.

"News flash!" Wally said. "The whole world doesn't want to be an actor, you know."

"Well, if you're into being a musician so much, why'd you put 'Dentist' on your index card for the hall bulletin board?" I'd been meaning to bring that up.

"I dunno," he said, wiping the sweat off his forehead. "My dad's a dentist."

"Oh, well, that makes sense," I said, 'cause it obviously didn't. "Whatever."

I whacked the poster up on the side of a telephone booth, and we continued walking at a faster pace.

"You know, sometimes people do stuff just to make other people happy," he said. "You should try it sometime."

Wally sped up and stayed about a half a block ahead of me until we got to the corner of Chugwater and Spruce. That's where we always split off in different directions.

"Here, take these – I'm not putting 'em up," Wally said, handing me his stack of posters. "That play is just a freakin' waste of time. I've got better things to do."

"So, what does that mean?" I asked. "Are you quitting?"

"I'll get back to you on that."

"That's what you said about the party!" I wanted to sock him, but I held back. "I need an answer right now," I said as calmly as I could. "Are you quitting, or what?"

"Maybe I am, and maybe I – *am!*"

"Fine! Have a nice life," I hollered, and tore down Chugwater.

"Fine!" Wally said, heading up Spruce.

A few seconds later I heard him call out to me, "Oh, by the way – about your play . . . ?"

I stopped to hear what he had to say without turning.

"I wish you all the luck in the world!"

Chapter 15

Gone Ape!

Trudging down Chugwater Road, I got a lungful of exhaust fumes from an oncoming Lotustown bus. It kicked off another one of my black-and-white movie memories: the night our whole family went to see Dad do his comedy act in Lotustown. I was around seven years old, I think. It was talent night in some little coffeehouse or something. Dad mainly talked about how crazy our family was: how Granny never bothered to close the door when she used the bathroom, and how birdbrained Aunt Birdie used air freshener for perfume 'cause she liked the smell. The family hated his "airing their dirty laundry," but the rest of the audience laughed. "Growing up Grubbs," Dad kept repeating. "And that's what it was like growing up –"

"Grubbs, Dustin Grubbs! Wait up!"

Oh, no. This is all I need right now.

LMNOP darted across Chugwater and ran to catch up with me, annoyingly cheerful as always.

"Great, we're both going in the same direction," she said, flashing her metal-mouth smile. "You're headed home, right? So now's the perfect time to talk, right?"

"Not really."

"Just so you know, I put up five posters already," she said, sliding her glasses up her nose. "One in the minimart at the gas station; one on the telephone booth at Cedar and Cubberly Place; one in Sow's Ear Antiques –"

"Okay, I get the picture!" I snapped.

I shifted gears into a power walk, but LMNOP had no problem keeping up with me. A clanking came from her backpack. It was probably jars filled with worm guts or something. I didn't want to know.

"I just bought some masking tape to put the posters up with," she said, "but you don't have to pay me back or anything. Oh, yeah! I put one in Finkelstein & Sons Hardware. That's four, right?"

"If you say so."

"Oh! And one in the Jukebox Café."

"Not now!" I yelled.

Some people aren't good at getting subtle signals, such as dirty looks and sharp answers. You have to whack them over the head with a two-by-four to get your point across. And even then –

"I hate to be a pain," she went on, "but my mom wants her plastic container back." And on and on and on. "Remember, the one that the brownies were in? It's part of a set."

"Uh-uh," I said, practically jogging.

"Hey, you'll never guess who I saw hanging out with Jeremy Jason Wilder at the Hinkleyville Mall," LMNOP said, panting and clanking beside me. "Guess! Guess who was hanging out with –"

"*Aaargh!*" I stopped short and slapped my hands over my ears, dropping the posters.

"What's wrong?" she squeaked.

"Stop it, Ellen!"

"Stop what?" Her eyes were darting back and forth.

A little voice in my head pleaded with me, *Don't do it! Just keep walking.* But my real voice drowned it out.

"Stop *this!* Stop stalking me, stop annoying me, stop trying to be my friend, okay?"

I'd never seen two eyes flood so fast. A fat tear streaked down her cheek. I should've ended it there, but I let my volcano erupt.

"You're *not* my friend, you're just my next-door neighbor. I saved your diseased cat once, about a million years ago, and I'm sorry I did, 'cause ever since then you won't stop bugging me! You're nothing but a *monumental pain!*"

I didn't know where all that came from. When the smoke in my head cleared, I saw LMNOP racing down the block. *Not my fault. That kid doesn't know when to let up!* But by the time I got home, I didn't like myself very much. I wished I could've taken everything back. I mean, if anybody knew all about the pain of rejection, it was yours truly.

For a second I thought I'd walked into the wrong house, 'cause ours was never so dark and quiet. Right house, just nobody home. I lumbered up the stairs and sat cross-legged on the living-room floor, chewing on a piece of dead thumbnail skin. *I'm pond scum. I didn't even thank her for buying the masking tape.* I ripped off a strip of skin with my teeth. It stung. Bled a little.

The phone rang and I jumped. Naturally, it was some girl calling for Gordy. Rebecca something-or-other. She didn't sound *too* gross. There was never any paper around, so I had to dig my spiral notebook out of my backpack to write down her info. Scrawled across the opposite page was Dad's cell-phone number – the one Aunt Olive had written down.

I knew I was going to call that number sooner or later. But later always seemed like the better choice. *Now is the perfect time. You're Dustin the Brave, right? And if you get too freaked out when you hear his voice, you can always just hang up.*

I ran to the window and back to make sure the coast was clear, limbering up my lips with a few rounds of "Unique New York." I picked up the phone and dialed. A woman's voice came through.

"Please press one or wait for the tone if you would like to leave a voice message for –"

"– Teddy Grubbs."

I hung up. (*Dustin the Dweeb.*) That was Dad's actual voice saying his own name. My heart was rattling something awful. *I should probably think about what I'm going to say first.* Should I shoot for a casual/friendly message? "Hi, it's me, Dustin. Just calling to shoot the breeze." Urgent/formal? "This is your youngest son, Dustin Grubbs. I need to speak to you ASAP!" Happy/curious? Bitter/direct?

Too many choices. Just wing it!

I took a gigantic breath and redialed.

"Hello, it's Dustin . . . Grubbs," I said after the message, the choices, and the beep. "Uh, Aunt Olive gave me your number, so I thought I'd try to call and say hi. I hope that's okay. So I guess that's it. Just hi. Okay, bye."

That two-second call probably took ten years off my life.

At school the next day, Wally acted as if I had the bubonic plague. But I wasn't going to cave and make the first move again, no matter what. I had my pride. I'd have my jaw wired shut if I had to. But he caught me off guard when he showed up for play rehearsal.

"What are you doing here?" I said.

I didn't expect an answer, and I didn't get one. Later on I

overheard part of his explanation to Cynthia Zimmerman. Something about "my parents made me," "finishing what I started," and "just steering clear of that selfish jerk."

"Before we get to the blocking, kiddles," Miss Van Rye said, "I'd like everyone to choose the animal that most reminds you of the character you're portraying. This is a fabulous exercise for making your characters really come alive."

I picked a chimpanzee, 'cause Jingle Jangles was always bouncing off the walls. I really got into it. By the time Miss Van Rye shouted, "Scene!" I found myself attempting to swing from the curtain ropes. I caught Wally laughing, but as soon as he saw me looking he stopped.

After rehearsal I was waiting for Pepper to get some junk from the girls' locker room so I could help her carry it home. I think she was cleaning out her gym locker or something. That's when Jeremy snuck up on me from behind.

"Dusty, my man," he said. "Awesome monkey, banana-breath!"

"Your snake was good too."

Okay, why is he being so friendly all of a sudden?

"You are totally insane!" he said, throwing his arm around my shoulder.

I think he meant that in a good way.

"Bye, guys," Cynthia said on her way out. "Dustin, you're gonna steal the show!"

"Thanks. Hey, did you ever do acting exercises like these

before?" I asked Jeremy. I hated to admit it to myself, but I wanted our conversation to keep going. He was being pretty decent to me during rehearsals, which was more than I could say for the Walrus. Oh, Jeremy was moody and snobby for sure, but I chalked that up to living in Hollywood his whole life and then being dragged out to Buttermilk Falls.

"No way," he said. "We were lucky if we had our lines memorized. You're always racing against time on a sitcom."

"Wow," I said. "Pressure."

Wally rushed by and gave us a dirty look. He slammed the door so hard when he left that the windowpanes rattled.

"What's his problem?" Jeremy said, loading his black and brown suede backpack, which matched his jacket perfectly. (I didn't point it out, but the price tag was still on his sleeve.) "Just between you and me," he said, "I think this stuff Van Rye's putting us through is a bunch of bull hockey."

"So why are you even doing the play?" I said. "Did Futterman promise to graduate you a year early or something?"

"I've got my reasons," Jeremy said. "Trust me."

We pushed open the big metal door that led outside to the top of the stone steps. It was still light enough that we had to squint after coming out of the dark auditorium.

"Don't you miss it?" I asked.

"What?"

"Being on television?"

"I guess. But my series lasted for four straight years," Jeremy said. "Been there, done that. I'm aiming for the big screen, baby!"

"I hear ya. So why Buttermilk Falls?"

"Good question. Ask my parents."

I heard music. It turned out to be Jeremy's cell phone/camera/minicomputer. I swear it actually played the first six notes of "Hooray for Hollywood" instead of ringing.

"Talk to me," he said instead of hello. "Yeah, just now. Lame. I'll tell you later. Where are you? Tammy's House of what? You're cutting out. Well, how long? Five minutes? Okay, bye. On the Spruce Street side. Yeah, bye."

He flipped the phoneamajig closed and slid it into his jacket pocket.

"Evelyn'll be here any minute," he said. "Can we give you a lift?"

"Oh, that's okay. I'm waiting for Pepper." I peeked through the window in the door. "I don't know why it's taking so long to clean out a gym locker."

"Whatever."

"Maybe the fumes from her gym clothes knocked her out cold," I said. "Nah, the stink factor is definitely a lot lower with girls."

"Funny," Jeremy said without smiling. "So how'd you get to be so hilarious?"

"It's probably genetic. My dad –" I stopped myself. *I don't want to get into the whole Dad thing.* "Well, you've met my family – I probably have monkey blood in me." I pulled my ears out and gave him my best "ooh-ooh aah-aah eeeee!"

"You're hysterical," Jeremy said, snorting. "You're like Dustin Grubbs, One-Man Show!"

The day before, Jeremy would barely look at me, and now he was shooting off compliments and offering me rides home. In real life he was a lot like the *Double Take* twins he played on TV. One day, nasty like Buddy Bickford; the next day, friendly like Bailey Bickford. Typecasting.

"Do the whole monkey thing again, Dusty. That cracked me up."

"I'm all monkeyed out."

"Oh, come on. Do it!"

"*You* do it," I said.

I couldn't believe it. Jeremy launched into a bad imitation of me imitating a monkey. Armpit-scratching, the whole nine yards.

"Funny!" I said, 'cause how could I not?

He stopped suddenly when Travis Buttrick came tearing down the street on his mountain bike.

"Real cool, Jer," Travis yelled. He slowed down long enough to spit a giant loogie onto the curb. "See what happens when you hang out with retards?"

We both ignored him and Travis pedaled off, popping a wheelie. Jeremy took a pair of chrome sunglasses out of his pocket, cleaned them on his shirttail, and slid them on.

"You look like you're having a blast playing the Jester," he said quietly. "Not that the Prince isn't a juicy role – it's probably the most well written in the whole play."

"You think?" I said.

Jeremy leaned up against the wall like he was doing it a favor.

"Think about it. This dude comes on the scene looking good, talking pretty, right? And then *bam!*" He punched the palm of his hand, and I flinched. "He turns out to be the bad guy."

"Hmm, I guess you're right," I said.

"Not much of a stretch for me, though," he said, running his fingers through his hair in one smooth movie-star move. "Sometimes an actor needs a little challenge."

A car pulled up in front of the school and honked.

"Here she is." Jeremy grabbed his backpack and hopped down a few steps. "Uh, this is a rental. Our Porsche is being detailed."

"Hey, I wouldn't know a Porsche from a porch."

"Funny man," he said. "Are you sure we can't drop you? Come on. To heck with Pepper."

"No, she'll pound me."

"Okay, then. Later."

Jeremy glided down the steps and slipped into the passenger seat of the car.

"The play is gonna get a lot of attention, thanks to me," he said, poking his head out of the window. "You'll see. Ciao!"

The window rolled up and the car sped off, leaving a trail of black smoke down Spruce Street. I watched the car get smaller and smaller until the covered bridge on Claremont swallowed it up.

I sat on the top step, thinking about what Jeremy'd said. It had never occurred to me before that the role of the Prince was all that hot. *Am I missing something?* I took out my script and flipped through it. *I can see his point. The Prince is a cool part.* But when I put it to the ultimate test, it failed. *Prince Krispen has exactly thirty-six lines – not even close to the Jester's whopping ninety-seven.*

"What gives?" Pepper said. She was standing in the door-way, holding two full plastic garbage bags. "I thought you left without me."

"I was talking to Jeremy," I said.

"Ugh! What did he want?"

"Nothing much. You know, he can be really nice when he wants to. He even offered me a ride. Didn't want to take no for an answer."

"Well, obviously he did."

"Did what?"

"Take no for an answer," Pepper said.

"What have you got in those things?" I said. "You're like Mrs. Sternhagen with her shopping bags."

"Best behavior, Mr. Grubbs!" she said, dropping one of the bags next to me. "Coach Mockler was dumping out a bunch of old equipment – knee pads, grungy softballs. I figured my stepdad could sell 'em in the yard sale he's having. You can carry the smaller bag."

"You're *too* kind," I said.

I unzipped my backpack to put my script away and a piece of paper fell out. I picked it up and unfolded it. It wasn't my math quiz, as I'd thought. It was from the *Tattletaler,* one of those tabloid newspapers they sell at grocery-store checkouts.

"What's that?" Pepper said.

"Dunno," I said. DOUBLE TAKE STAR IS DOUBLE TROUBLE! the headline read. "I think it's an article about Jeremy!"

"Read it!"

I began speed-reading the two-page article out loud while we lugged the lumpy bags up Spruce Street.

After months of putting up with Jeremy Jason Wilder's tantrums on the set of his sitcom, producers threatened to pull the plug on next year's season. "He's gone through six tutors since the show began three years ago," Jonathan Michaels, the show's executive producer, told us. "And we've just lost the seventh. We're bending over backward to meet Jeremy's demands, but enough is enough!" When asked to respond to these harsh accusations, representatives for the twelve-year-old Wilder had no comment.

"That doesn't sound like the Jeremy we know," Pepper said.

"You're right," I said. "The Jeremy we know told us he was eleven."

"No, I mean he's kind of stuck up and quiet."

"Wait! This newspaper is a year old, so now he must be around thirteen!"

"Weird," Pepper said. "Then why is he still in sixth grade? Keep reading!"

The sitcom star's mother, Evelyn Wilder, a former child actress herself, broke down in tears when she spoke about Jeremy. "He's really a good kid, but he's going through a lot right now, at home and at the studio. People just don't understand all the pressure he's under."

"Then there's more about infantile behavior . . . violating his contract . . . lawsuit pending. . . ."

"Jeez, if all this is true," Pepper said, flicking the paper, "how come we didn't hear about it on *Show-Biz Beat?*"

"I remember hearing some stuff. Nothing this bad, though."

The picture of Jeremy they'd printed with the article showed his mouth wide open and his fists in the air. *You can't trust the tabloids. It looks like a still shot from the* Double Take *episode when he sat on a hornet's nest.*

"You know what the real mystery is?" I said, catching my breath.

"What?"

"How did this get into my script? Somebody must've snuck it in when I wasn't looking. But who?"

"Let's take a breather," Pepper said, dropping her bag and plopping down on the bench in front of Finkelstein & Sons Hardware. "Not that I need one."

I dropped my bag too and collapsed onto the bench next to her. Pepper folded her hands on top of her head, as if she were giving careful thought to my question.

"Well, it had to be someone in the play, right?" she said. "Maybe Darlene – she's always sticking her nose into everybody else's business."

"This whole thing reeks of Wally, if you ask me."

"Makes sense."

We both propped our feet up on the garbage bags and sat there thumbing through the rest of the tabloid pages.

"Hey, Pep," I said, snickering, "I guess if we believe this stuff about Jeremy, then we have to buy the story on the other side of it too."

"What's it say?"

"'Two-Headed Man Runs for Mayor . . . against Himself!'"

Chapter 16

Guess Who's Coming to Dinner?

If real life were a sitcom, mine would sound something like this:

DUSTIN. Hey, if anybody cares, I'm home!
GORDY. Nobody cares.
[**Canned laughter**]
MOM. Dustin, you're late.
GORDY. Yeah, dork.
DUSTIN. Juvenile delinquent! I waited around to help Pepper carry some junk home, Mom.
GORDY. That's about the best you can do. A girl who thinks she's a boy.
DUSTIN. Jealous! Better than hanging with pizza-face Edith, playing with her barbed-wire collection.
[**Canned laughter**]

[**Gordy gets Dustin in a headlock.**]

GORDY. Take it back!

DUSTIN. Eeeoow, you have diarrhea breath! Mom, help!

MOM. Gordon, let go of your brother — now! This isn't the zoo.

GORDY. He belongs in a zoo.

DUSTIN. Oh, good one, braniac. What would we do without Gordy's sense of humor? Gordy, what do **you** do without it?

[**Canned laughter**]

GORDY. Same thing you're gonna do without your face when I rip it off.

DUSTIN. That doesn't even make sense.

[**Canned laughter**]

MOM. Come on, guys, I don't have time for this. Company's coming! [**Looking up to the heavens**] Why did I have to have boys?

That's pretty close to the way it actually went down, anyway. But one thing's for sure – real life would be a lot easier with a laugh track and commercial breaks.

Back to reality: Gordy wouldn't let go of me, so Mom threatened to get the broom. Not to whack us with or to sweep up ripped-off body parts with or anything – she'd always get black-and-blue marks when she tried to pry us apart, so she'd started using a broom to do it instead. That was the usual drill. But this time the fighting just petered out after Gordy asked, "What company?"

"Barry Ortega, from the Donut Hole," Mom said. "I thought he should get to know the two of you a little better. So we're going to have a nice, relaxing dinner – just the four of us. We're having spaghetti."

"No fair, springing this on us out of the blue," Gordy said.

For once I agree with Gordo. Are things heating up between Mom and the Donut King? That'd be bad enough, but do we have to watch him eat?

The table was set with the good dishes, and cloth napkins instead of paper towels, but that wasn't going to matter. Mom was still a lousy cook. It was no coincidence that with all the homemade food at Granny's party, Mom's only responsibility was plastic plates and cups.

"Why the sour faces?" Mom said. "I made your aunt Olive's meatballs that I had in the freezer. Dustin, you love your aunt Olive's meatballs."

That explained the yummy smells coming from the kitchen.

"Now, change into something decent, you two," Mom said, rushing into the living room. "He'll be here any minute!" As if my tuxedo T-shirt and cargo shorts weren't good enough for dinner at Chez Grubbs.

Mr. Ortega – Barry – showed up right on time with a box of Jack Sprat doughnuts and a bunch of daisies. After celery, carrots, and onion dip in the living room, we all sat around the kitchen table. In silence.

"Barry's been working on some creative new ideas for jelly-filleds. Haven't you?" Mom finally said.

"That's right," Mr. Ortega said with a mouthful of salad. "Razzleberry! They'll be ready to go in about a week or two."

What the heck is a razzleberry? I thought, but smiled politely. Gordy gave him the evil eye.

"I'm testing out rhubarb filling too," Mr. Ortega said, all excited. "Oh, and I'm thinking about doing a combination of the two: razzle-barb. What do you think? I'm not sure it'll be a hit, but it's worth a shot, am I right?"

Gordy lined an olive pit at my head when no one was looking.

"Oww! Mom, Gordy's throwing stuff!"

"I wasn't sure it'd be a hit," he said, "but it was worth a shot, am I right?"

"Gordon!" Mom yelled.

"It slipped."

"Gordy got a tattoo!" I blurted out. "Oh, sorry – it slipped."

"So? Dustin's in a play!" Gordy fired back. "And he wants to be an actor when he grows up. *If* he grows up."

"What?" Mom said.

Weird how everything came spilling out all at once, like a busted piñata. That must've been the "juicy dirt" that Gordy said he had on me. Mom looked totally shocked. The veins in her neck were pulsing. I bit my lip, waiting for her to say something.

"Well," she finally said, buttering a bread stick, "we've certainly got a lot to discuss." The bread stick crumbled in her hand. "Later."

Mr. Ortega was crunching on more salad – quick little chomps, like an anxious rabbit gnawing his way out of a trap.

"But, Gordon, a tattoo?" Mom said, buttering another bread stick. "I can't believe you didn't even discuss it with me first." And bread stick number two bit the dust. "Where is it? Show me. No – never mind. Now is not the time."

"Why are you doggin' on *me*?" Gordy said with salad dressing dripping down his chin. "Didn't you hear what I said about Freakshow being in a play at school? And wanting to be an actor?"

"Oh, a few years ago he wanted to be a pony," Mom said, waving away his questions. "Dustin, I think it's wonderful that you're doing a play. Why didn't you tell me?"

"Huh?"

Maybe because I heard you say stuff like "The day your father stepped onto a stage was the day this family started falling apart." That's all.

But I just shrugged. An ocean of relief washed over me. Keeping secrets from Mom wasn't easy. If I'd known she was gonna be all for it, I could've saved myself a whole lot of hassle.

"I have the lead too," I said, smirking at Gordy.

"The lead in your school play?" Mr. Ortega said. "Well, that sounds like fun. You be sure to reserve two front-row seats for your mom and me on opening night."

Slick, how he tried to weasel his way into another date with Mom.

"It's good to have a hobby like that when you're a kid that you can really sink your teeth into," Mr. Ortega said. "I remember I used to love collecting baseball cards. Still have 'em. They might actually be worth something now."

"Acting isn't just a hobby," I said. "I'm gonna be a professional someday."

"Get real!" Gordy said. "Who'd pay money to see your ugly mug?"

"I'll bet you dollars to doughnuts that you'll see things differently when you're a little older," Mr. Ortega said, stabbing the largest meatball on the serving platter and plopping it onto his plate. "I'm not gonna sugarcoat it. That's a real hard life, being an actor – filled with rejection. So they say, anyway."

"Uh-huh," I muttered. "Well, I'm used to it."

It was time to move on to another subject. Frosting and sprinkles, maybe. But Mr. Ortega kept yammering on and on about acting as if he knew what he was talking about.

"You have to move to one of the coasts – to L.A. or New York. And you have to have a lot of talent – not that you don't – and plenty of just plain luck."

"I guess it'd be easier to stay in Buttermilk Falls forever and think up new shapes for doughnuts or something. But some of us have bigger dreams!" Okay, that's just what I was thinking. What came out was "I know all that." My attempt at making polite dinner conversation was officially over.

"Well, he's got plenty of time to think about a career, for goodness' sake," Mom said, popping up from her chair. "More gravy, Barry?"

My whole family called it gravy, even though the rest of the world called it sauce – *spaghetti* sauce.

"Please."

"It's out of a jar," she confessed, ladling sauce over his mushy spaghetti. "But I added extra basil and oregano."

"Everything is just delicious, Dot. First rate."

"Dot"? They already have pet names for each other? Does she call him Boo-Boo Barry? Or honey bear? Or my-great-big-cuddly-wuddly-bear-claw-with-sugar-on-top?

Another thick silence hung over us like a rain cloud ready to burst. Mr. Ortega's face was shiny with flop sweat. I watched his enormous Adam's apple rise and fall, and it made me think of the New Year's Eve ball in Times Square – without the celebration.

He reached for a piece of cement garlic bread, took a bite, and then scratched the back of his head. That was when I noticed it: his hair was crooked. Mr. Ortega was wearing a toupee! Two meatballs later, Gordy noticed it too.

"By the way, I had a really nice time at the birthday party, Dot," Mr. Ortega finally said. "Thanks for inviting me."

"Oh, I'm glad you could make it."

"Your mother-in-law is quite a character," he said.

His part was at an angle and a little piece of netting was showing over his left ear.

"Yeah, remember when Gran spilled the red wine?" Gordy said. His eyes were dancing. "We still can't get the stain out of the rug."

"Gordon," Mom said, glaring.

"What?"

"Uh – pass me the Parmesan cheese."

"Sure thing, Dot," Gordy said, handing her the jar. He was a master at keeping a straight face.

Mom stared Gordy down while she sprinkled the stinky-feet-smelling cheese over her spaghetti.

"More cheese, Barry?"

"Can't get enough of the stuff," he said, chuckling.

Mom passed the Parmesan to Mr. Ortega. After a few sprinkles, he shook the jar and spanked the bottom.

"Looks like you're all out," he said.

"Oh, well," Gordy said. "Hair today, gone tomorrow."

I almost lost it. Mom slammed her fork on the table and flaming darts shot out of her eyes, straight into Gordy's forehead.

There was only the clinking sound of silverware against plates. Soon Mr. Ortega and his hair were facing in two different directions, and he didn't have a clue. It was hard not to stare and even harder not to crack up, but I knew I'd be okay as long as his hair didn't land on his plate. But Gordy wouldn't let up.

"So, Barry," he said, "how would you get, say, razzleberry stains out of *your* rug?"

I laughed and gasped at the same time. Somehow a strand of spaghetti got sucked up into my head and was on its way out of my nose! I didn't even know that was humanly possible!

I wanted to give the noodle one good yank, but I was afraid it'd rupture and I'd have to have it surgically removed. My eyes were tearing up. I breathed through my mouth and tugged – and tugged. Spaghetti sauce was scorching my brain as I carefully pulled the noodle out of my right nostril. Like nasal floss.

The spaghetti strand ended up back on my plate again, totally white and in one whole piece. It was amazing that it had made the journey without breaking.

A mouthful of cola sprayed out of Gordy's mouth. He pounded on the table, busting a gut. "You should do *that* in your show!" he said. "I'd pay money to see that again!"

The Donut King had a glazed look on his face. Nobody was able to take another bite.

"Dustin, are you okay?" Mom asked.

I wasn't sure. My nose was on fire from the gravy/sauce with extra basil and oregano.

"It burns like crazy!" I said.

"Should I call nine-one-one?" she said. "Gordon, you are *not* helping!"

At this point Gordy was curled up in a ball on the floor, turning magenta. He'd reached the level of hysterical laughter at which it loses all sound.

"This could only happen to you, Dustin," Mom said, unrolling a mile of paper towels. "Here, blow! Blow!"

But blowing my nose didn't put out the fire. I ran to the refrigerator and stuck my face in the freezer. That didn't help either. Mom grabbed my arm and pulled me to the sink. We had to step over Gordy on the way.

"Keep rinsing your nostrils with cool water," she said. "That should do the trick."

Relief! The water felt so good I stuck my whole head under the faucet and gargled. Over the sound of the water I could hear Gordy moaning in pain from laughing too hard. I pulled my head out of the sink and Mom ran to get me a towel from the bathroom. Mr. Ortega was still sitting there, clutching the side of the table as if he were on Mr. Toad's Wild Ride.

"Get used to it," I said to him, pounding water out of my ear. "This is what it's like growing up Grubbs!"

Chapter 17

Cahoots

Aunt Olive was gushing. She told me she'd spoken to Dad from her job at the bakery and that: "He's excited to talk to you! But he thinks it'd be best if *you* called *him* again – but not on his cell. It's on the fritz." He was doing a gig at the Punch Line Palace, in Chicago – a three-hour train ride from Buttermilk Falls. She gave me the number, plus five dollars in quarters, and told me to call on a public telephone any time after five. "But please don't tell your mother, or she'll have me tarred and feathered."

At 4:43, I pocketed the quarters and my keys (which were now attached to that star key chain that Dad had given me) and jangled all the way to the pay phone on Cubberly. There was a show poster hanging on it, one that LMNOP had taped up. My finger was shaking so bad that I misdialed twice.

"Yes, may I please speak to Theodore Grubbs – Teddy Grubbs?" I said when a man answered the phone. "Sure, I'll hold."

I was on hold forever, suffocating in that booth. I caught a whiff of the half-eaten pizza slice that was smooshed on the ground, and those old familiar water balloons began sloshing around in my stomach again. But I had a feeling that once I heard Dad's voice I'd be okay. It was probably a lot like stage fright – as soon as you get your first few lines out, the panic disappears.

"What's that?" I could barely hear, it was so noisy. "He's not in yet?"

Shoot!

"Yeah, sure, you can take a message, I guess," I said, raising my voice over the racket. "Tell him – tell him that his son Dustin –"

"Please insert sixty cents for the next three minutes," a voice interrupted.

Ugh! I dug three more quarters out of my pocket and popped them into the slot, fumbling the last one. I was trying to think of all the info I needed to include in my message. I'm pretty sure I got it all out in one breath.

"Tell him that Dustin is doing the lead in a play called *The Castle of the Crooked Clowns* – no, *Crooked Crowns* – uh, you really don't have to give him the name – of the play, I mean, but it's on May first at eight p.m. in the school auditorium. And tell him that I'll go ahead and reserve a seat for him, just in case he's in the area."

Gasp.

"That's Saturday, May first, at eight!"

I doubted he'd show up. He might not even get the message. It was worth a shot.

The last thing you need when your life is a frazzled mess is to be forced into something you're not cut out for. Gym class was complete torture for me – let me count the ways. First off, the locker room smelled like feet. Second, there was all that public undressing going on. I always beat the other boys to the locker room so I could change in private. (Scrawny kids shouldn't have to advertise it.) Third, they hadn't invented a sport that I was even kinda-sorta good at.

I pulled my T-shirt off the top shelf of my gym locker and something fell out. A note:

JEREMY AND TRAVIS Buttrick ARE iN cAHootS!
BEWARE!

                                  – A FORMER FRIEND

First the tabloid pages, now this? Beware of what? Jeremy and I were getting along great lately, and I'd never even seen him give Butthead the time of day.

I looked up *cahoots* in my pocket dictionary just to be sure.

Ca • hoots (ke-hoots) *pl. n. Informal.* Questionable collaboration; secret partnership: *an accountant in* cahoots *with organized crime.*

[Perhaps from French *cahute,* cabin, from Old French, possibly blend of *cabane;* see CABIN, and *hutte.* See HUT.]

Now, who was this "former friend"? *Hmm, let's see. A Jeremy Jason Wilder hater who's allowed in the boys' locker room. Duh. The Walrus strikes again! Case closed.*

"Dusty, my man! Drop and give me twenty."

It was Jeremy. See? Friendly, nice. The total opposite of Travis Buttrick.

"Hey, Jer," I said. I flung the note into my locker and banged the door shut.

"Are we shooting hoops today?" he asked.

"I'm not sure."

I never paid attention to what Coach Mockler said we'd be doing in our next class. I didn't want to spend sleepless nights worrying about it.

Jeremy changed into his gym clothes, and we sat facing each other on the long wooden bench, tying our sneakers. It was a good thing I noticed the bottom of my shoe before Jeremy did. Wally had gone too far. Drawn on the sole of my right sneaker in black marker was a giant

I slapped my feet on the ground so Jeremy wouldn't see. He was busy stashing a roll of cash in his sock anyway. *Celebrities!*

"Gum?" Jeremy asked, holding out a pack.

"Nuh-uh. We have class in, like, two minutes."

"So? It's just gym." He threw me a piece, which, of course, I missed. "In case you change your mind."

I had to admit, being friends with a TV star had its advantages. Even a stupid conversation with him made you feel important somehow. I picked up the gum. Grape-flavored Chubby Bubble? I thought he'd chew some sort of imported designer gum.

"Can I ask you something?" Jeremy said. "It's about the play."

"Shoot."

"Well, I've been thinking about it and – well, the Prince is kind of a small part. Great, but small."

"And?"

I didn't like where this was heading.

"Okay, I'll cut to the chase." Jeremy shot up and put one foot on the bench. "I think we should trade parts – you can be the Prince, and I'll be the Jester."

Wow! I didn't see that one coming.

"Face it," he said, cracking his knuckles, "people are only coming to see this turkey because of me. They're gonna ask for their money back if I'm barely in it, right?"

I stared up at him. Words rushed to my mouth, but none came out.

"C'mon, we have a whole week of rehearsal left," Jeremy said. He popped his gum. "That's plenty of time to learn new roles." *Pop! Snap!* "You said you had all the parts memorized anyway, so it's no big deal, right?" *Smack!*

Anger rose up my spine like mercury in a boiling thermometer.

Jeremy spat the wad of gum out and stuck it under the bench. "Flavor's gone already," he said. I should've reported him to Coach Mockler for vandalism.

"I'll think about it," I muttered, but I didn't really mean it.

"There's nothing to think about, buddy," he said, slapping my back. "Futterman and Van Rye already gave it the green light."

"What?"

"Thanks a lot, Dusty," he said. "You're a real pro."

"Dustin."

"Huh?"

"My name is Dustin."

"Okay, no problem," Jeremy said, and drifted into the gym.

If I were a cartoon character, steam would've blown out of both my ears. *He can't be the Jester! He's about as funny as a swift knee to the groin!* I got up and kicked the heck out of the water fountain, then collapsed onto the bench.

Oh, who am I kidding? The school wouldn't even be doing the play at all right now without his star power.

The locker room was filling up with the other boys from my class, who were laughing and locker slamming. I lined the piece of Chubby Bubble across the room.

"Grubbs!" Coach Mockler said, coming out of his office. "Use the trash receptacle."

He blew his whistle. Class was starting, so I followed the rest of the boys into the gymnasium. Mockler had us stand in one long line while he took attendance and divided us into teams. Jeremy was a head taller than the rest of us – not to mention almost old enough to vote. I squeezed in next to Wally.

"Thanks for the note," I whispered. "You might be right."

"What note?" Wally snarled.

"C'mon, 'former friend,' I know it was you. In my locker – the note, the sneakers –"

"I'm still not speaking to you, so quit making me speak."

"Okay, listen up!" Coach Mockler said. "I'm scouting new recruits for next year's Fireballs, so I'm going to be watching you guys like a hawk today."

The Buttermilk Falls Fireballs was our seventh- and eighth-grade boys' basketball team. Everybody called them the Butterballs.

"Okay, guys, count off by twos, starting with Plunket." Mockler blew four short whistle blasts to set the tempo.

"Jeremy just dropped a bomb on me," I told Wally. The line was shouting "one, two, one, two," so I didn't need to whisper anymore. "He wants to trade parts."

"So?" Wally said. "Shut up or we'll get in trouble. *One!*"

"He's such a – *two!* – face. And what's the deal with him and Travis?"

"I don't know what you're talking about."

"Okay, listen up!" Mockler said again. "It's the Shirts against the Skins. The ones are the Shirts; the twos are the Skins. Got it?"

"I forgot what I am," I said.

"I'm Shirts," Wally said, "so you're Skins. Too bad, so sad."

"Oh, man!"

Me and the other Skins stripped down and threw our T-shirts on the bleachers. Being forced to play sports was bad enough, but having to be half-naked at the same time was just "adding insult to injury," as Aunt Olive says.

Mockler tossed the basketball into the air and everyone went for it like lions to fresh kill. *Let the fun begin!* The sounds of the ball bouncing and sneakers squeaking echoed off the gym walls while I ran into the outfield, or the end zone, or whatever it's called. I'd learned from experience that it was best to steer clear of the kids who actually knew what they were doing.

Jeremy was the first to try for a basket. He leaped three feet into the air, heaving the ball clear across the gym. It missed.

"Ha-ha!" I said. I think Jeremy heard, 'cause he shot me a dirty look.

The more I thought about it, the more I realized that he'd been setting me up the whole time. *"The Prince is a juicy role – the most well written in the whole play."* The tabloids were right – he really was a spoiled brat.

Some idiot threw me the ball. Somehow I caught it. I was going to toss it right back, but Mockler was looking my way, so I danced around a little and grunted. Suddenly I was drowning in a blur of armpits and grabby hands.

"Dribble!" someone yelled as I charged across the floor, gripping the basketball. "Dribble!"

I wiped a hand across my mouth, but I wasn't drooling. *What is he yelling about?*

"Bounce the freakin' ball!" Reggie MacPherson, one of the Skins, shouted.

Okay, I can do that. I bounced it once. Twice. Couldn't keep it going. A clump of Shirts was attacking, so I closed my eyes and hurled the ball up toward the orange hoop.

I heard cheering.

"Did I make it?" I asked, opening my eyes. "Did I score points?"

"Yeah, two," Reggie said, "for the other team! Wrong basket, meathead!"

Okay, that was it – back to the sidelines. Can't say I didn't try. After a lot more jumping around, some kids started yelling, "Foul! Out of bounds!" Mockler gave his whistle a sharp blast.

"Free throw!" he shouted. "Plunket, you're up!"

The game came to a standstill. All eyes were on Felix, who stared up at the basket, holding the ball as if it were made of precious glass.

"Don't freeze up, Felix!" someone shouted.

"Yeah, d-d-d-don't freak out like you did in that stupid p-p-p-p-play!"

Who knew that another kid besides me was still suffering from the aftereffects of the play? Poor Felix was standing there, sweating buckets, just like when he was the Prince. But he shut everyone up when he made the basket.

"Way to go, Felix!" I shouted.

Reggie shoved me.

"I know, I know, he's on the other team."

Mockler called a break, and everyone crowded around the water fountain.

"Nice shot," I said, catching up to Felix. His sweat smelled like chicken soup.

"Thanks," he said.

"I can't believe people are still teasing you about the play."

"Tell me about it," he said, wiping his face on his T-shirt. "I was practically guaranteed a spot in the F-F-Fireballs next year, but I think I blew it when the coach saw me freeze up on that stage. Now he knows I crack under pressure."

"That's not fair. You're a great basketball player."

"Even though that play was the worst thing that ever happened to me, I wish I had another shot at it," Felix said. "A do-over."

Wally was sucking the water fountain dry, and Brian Flabner gave him a poke.

"C'mon, Tubbo," he said. "Save some for the fish."

Wally turned around and squirted a mouthful of water at him – only it hit Jeremy instead.

"Hey, watch it!" Jeremy yelled. His sneakers were soaked. "These cost a fortune. Jerk!"

"Jeez, lighten up, it's only water," I said.

"They're brand new, okay?"

"Sorry," Wally said. "I'll get some paper towels."

"Too bad Mr. Hollywood can't buy himself a little coordination," Reggie said to Brian. "Maybe we'd be winning."

Mockler blew his whistle. We all took quick slurps of water and rushed back onto the gym floor.

As soon as the game started, Mockler disappeared into his office and Jeremy took off with the ball. I don't know what got into him, but he was spinning the ball on his finger, bouncing it through his legs backward, sideways, really going nuts.

"What's he trying to prove?" I said loud enough for Jeremy to hear.

I couldn't stand to watch anymore, so I crouched down to retie my laces. Something slammed into me. Hard. The next thing I knew, Jeremy was on the floor, tangled up in himself like a broken umbrella.

"Hey, man," I said. "Are you all right?"

"Do I look all right?" he yelled. "My leg! Ohh, my *leeeg!*"

"Let's help him up," Wally said, reaching for his arm.

"No!" Felix said, pulling Wally back. "Don't you know you're not supposed to move somebody after they've f-f-f-fallen? You could do serious damage."

"I turn my back for two minutes!" Mockler said, jogging over to us with a first-aid kit. "What the heck happened here?"

"It was an accident," I said.

"Or *not!*" Jeremy snapped.

"MacPherson, run and get Nurse Opal," Mockler said. "Pronto!"

"I don't want that cow touching me!" Jeremy hollered. "Get my cell phone from the locker room – I'm paging Evelyn." Then he pointed at me and said, "And get him outta my sight!"

It looked as if he was showing his true colors – and they weren't just black and blue.

I was pretty miserable until the next day, when Miss Honeywell told me that something "scrumptious" was waiting for me in the main office. I thought the secretary had baked her nonfat lemon bars again, but it was even better. It turned out to be a telegram addressed to Mr. Dustin T. Grubbs, "Star!," c/o Buttermilk Falls Elementary. The only telegrams I'd ever seen were in old backstage movie musicals. I didn't even think they existed anymore.

"I'm there, son. STOP" was all it said.

That was enough. I was psyched.

Chapter 18

The Royal Flush

The cast of the play was in a wide-eyed clump hanging out of the first-floor windows of Miss Van Rye's kindergarten classroom – and hanging on every word that was being said outside. Even though I was stuck playing the stupid Prince, it was still the most exciting night of my life. Heck, Hollywood was in our own backyard!

"This is *Show-Biz Beat* special correspondent Callie Sinclair, reporting from the steps of Buttermilk Falls Elementary School in the quaint midwestern town of the same name. Tonight we're kicking off our weeklong series *Whatever Happened to My Favorite Celebrity Kids?* in which we'll be conducting interviews with child stars who have disappeared from the spotlight. We're here at a special performance of a play called *The Castle of the Cracked Crowns,* a fund-raiser featuring Jeremy Jason Wilder –"

Screams gushed out of a crowd of girls surrounding Callie.

"Cut! Cut!" A short man in a *Show-Biz Beat* jacket made a throat-slashing gesture. "They keep drowning you out every time you say Jeremy Jason –"

"*Jeremeee!*" the crowd squealed.

"Okay, you maniacs, work with me here!" the man shouted.

"Take it easy, Phil," Callie said. "It's only a dry run."

"But we'll be taping it next time around!" He turned to the swarm of girls. "Okay, ladies," he said, switching to a sugary voice. "I'm the director, so I'm going to give you a little direction. First, can everyone take a giant step backward? Good. Super. Brilliant. Now I need all of you to be perfect little angels and *shut up!*"

A lady wearing a *Show-Biz Beat* jacket rushed over to Callie and fogged her with hair spray.

"There's a typo in the copy, Cal," the director said. A guy holding an open notebook was whispering in his ear. "It's *Crooked Crowns* – not *Cracked*. Okay, clear it, Flo! Cal, whenever you're ready."

"Three, two – This is *Show-Biz Beat* special corr–"

"Sorry," another guy in headsets interrupted. "We're picking up the wind."

The techie slipped a spongy blue cover over Callie's microphone while she glanced through the pages in her hand.

"Okay, you're good to go!" he said.

"The *Double Take* star will be performing tonight in spite of a recent leg injury. The irrepressible" – Callie looked at the crowd, then back at her pages – "the irrepressible you-know-who was quoted as saying, 'A little thing like a fractured tibia and some torn cartilage ain't gonna stop me from helping my school.' What a remarkable young man!"

The director made a spinning motion with his hand.

"This is certainly a turnaround for hmm-hmm-hmm, whose rumored tantrums on the set forced network execs to cancel his popular 'hitcom,'" Callie said, picking up the pace. "We'll be backstage later on for an exclusive interview with Jeremy Jason Wilder. Oops!"

The crowd screeched even louder than before.

I closed one of the windows halfway, careful not to get soot on my Prince costume. It was the one Felix had worn, which was way too long but a heck of a lot nicer than the pillowcase tunic that Mrs. Dorkin had made me. I decided to wear the belt I'd made from Dad's neckties with it too.

"Come on, you guys," I said to the cast, "you'd better get ready for the show."

"You're not in charge anymore," Wally snapped, still acting like a wiener.

"It's not even six o'clock," Darlene said. She went back to brushing her wig on its Styrofoam head. "We have hours before the curtain goes up."

"Callie Sinclair looks a lot older in person," Cynthia said, still peering out the window. "Don't you think?"

"She's still babe-alicious," Wally said. He shoved a stack of potato chips into his mouth and followed them up with a fistful of gummy worms.

"Gross!" Darlene said.

"I can't help it." Wally sucked in a dangling worm. "When I'm nervous, I eat."

"Hey, Dustin, are we gonna be on TV?" Pepper asked.

"I doubt it. They're just here for the interview."

"But it is a possibility," Darlene said, setting down her brush. "Omigod, all of a sudden I can't breathe!"

Jeremy appeared in the doorway leaning on an old man cane. Flung over his shoulder was a garment bag with Hollywood Costume Cavalcade printed on it. I thought that after his injury he'd drop out of the play for sure and I'd get my part back. No such luck.

"Hi, Jer. How's your leg?" I forced myself to say. I was making an effort to be as friendly as possible to him for the sake of the play. He just ignored me.

"Where did that mob out there come from?" he asked.

"Willowbridge, Lotustown, Hinkleyville," Millicent said, taking a break from chewing her hair. "We don't get many live celebrities in Buttermilk Falls."

"We don't get many dead ones either," Wally said, snorting.

"Good news, kiddles!" Miss Van Rye announced, prancing into the room. In her sparkly silver dress and matching turban, she looked like the world's largest disco ball. "Tonight's performance has been sold out since two o'clock – and now we're selling standing room to the Johnny-come-latelies. The box office is in such a tizzy. They're taking in money hand over fist!"

"They want me in costume for my interview," Jeremy muttered, looking unimpressed. "So, where do I get dressed?"

"The girls are changing behind the upright piano," Miss Van Rye said. She plopped down on the piano bench. "And the boys are behind the puppet theater."

Jeremy glanced at Wally's head, which was bobbing up and down behind a giant dragon puppet, and grabbed his garment bag.

"Uh, I don't think so," he said, hobbling toward the door. "I'll be in the boys' john."

"Okay, but don't dillydally," Miss Van Rye said. "We told *Show-Biz Beat* they could conduct your interview here at six-fifteen."

"Break a leg tonight, Jeremy!" Darlene called. The door slammed. "Oh, no – I meant that in a good way!"

"Heavens to Betsy," Miss Van Rye said, pumping the top of her dress for a breeze. Red blotches were sprouting up around her neck, forming a map of the United States. "I hope I don't pass out from the excitement."

"Poor Jeremy," Millicent cooed. "He can hardly walk."

"I wish he'd ditch the cane," Pepper said. "The Jester is supposed to be limber."

"And the Princess is supposed to be beautiful," Darlene said, turning on her.

"Don't start!" I yelled.

"Besides," Darlene went on, "the audience wouldn't care if he did the whole show lying down. He's Jeremy Jason Wilder!"

All the girls screamed and jumped around, imitating the crowd outside.

"Look! He forgot this," Millicent said, holding up a small plastic bag that matched the Hollywood Costume Cavalcade garment bag.

"Dustin, you're in costume already," Miss Van Rye said. "Why don't you be a prince and take it to him?" She cackled suddenly. "I mean, you are dressed the part!"

Don't rub it in, lady. After taking my starring role away and giving it to what's-his-face, she was definitely off my Christmas list.

Millicent handed me the bag. I pulled out a pair of striped tights and two perfect curly-toed jester's shoes with pompoms at the tips. When I was the Jester I wore my aunt Birdie's old house slippers, stuffed with newspaper.

"Quick like a bunny!" Miss Van Rye said, clapping. "And the rest of you should start getting dressed so we have time for a proper warm-up."

"No corks!" Darlene said.

I checked the boys' bathroom across from the kindergarten

classroom, but Jeremy wasn't there. *Why would he hobble all the way to the bathroom at the other end of the hall?* Crowds were already jamming the main entranceway near the auditorium. I tunneled my way through them and ended up smashed against the box-office door. While I was there I figured I'd pop in and do another quick check on my family's tickets. Miss Van Rye was right – it was chaos inside.

"Excuse me. Did my family arrive yet?" I asked politely. "Grubbs."

"You again?" one of the ladies barked. "Yes, yes, they just picked up the tickets."

"Great! Uh, did *all* the Grubbses' tickets get picked up?" The seat I'd reserved for Dad was away from the rest of my family – to avoid possible bloodshed if he actually showed up. "See, there were six in one envelope," I explained, "and then there was a single ticket in a separate –"

"Young man, can't you see we've got our hands full?" the lady said. "With you and that Jeremy Jason boy popping in and out every minute, you're driving us batty!"

"Sorry," I said, edging toward the door. My elbow knocked a metal box off a table. I quickly picked it up, put it back, and slipped into the hallway.

I decided to check for the gimp in the john at the deserted end of the hall. When I rounded the corner, I swear I saw someone who looked an awful lot like Jeremy running – not limping – into the boys' bathroom. *Bum leg, my foot!*

Just as I was about to barge in and accuse Jeremy of being a phony, I heard arguing coming from inside. *Stop!* I told myself. *Just listen.* I pressed my ear to the door.

"Did you get it?" a muffled voice said.

"Yeah, just now. It's in the stall with me." I could barely hear, but I thought it was Jeremy. "Listen, I don't have time to [something] it right now. I have to get sweaty."

That could've been "ready."

"I knew you could pull it off," the first voice said. "So fork it over."

"Listen, I'm not sure this was such a hot idea," Jeremy said. "If you could wait [something-something-something] return it and pay you back with my own money. I'm good for it. But if I get busted [something-something] in big trouble, Gladys."

The only Gladys I know is a cafeteria lady.

"Why the guilt trip all of a sudden? You said it yourself – they tricked you into this thing. They used your name to sell tickets, so the [something-something] is rightfully yours. Now, get your [something] out here, man."

"No!" Jeremy said.

I heard knocking that turned into pounding.

"We had a deal, and you're sticking to it!"

That wasn't Gladys. It was Travis – Buttrick! Jeremy and that lowlife really were in cahoots!

I pushed the door open a little and listened through the crack.

"Listen, Hollywood, who came crawling to who in the first

place?" Travis yelled. "I lent you as much as you wanted, and you agreed to pay me back by today, with interest. Forty percent! You put it in writing!"

"So sue me," Jeremy said.

"Grubbs! Where is Grubbs?"

Futterman was on a rampage, screaming my name in the hall. *Bad timing!* I flattened myself against the door, but it was too late. He was galloping right toward me.

"Jeremy, are you in here?" I said, rushing into the bathroom. "You forgot your shoes and tights. Oh, hi, Travis."

"None of your business," he growled, without my even asking anything.

"Okay, then," I said. "If anyone comes looking, I'm not here."

I hid in a corner of a doorless stall, wondering what I'd done this time to drive Futterman over the edge.

"All right, where is he?" Futterman shouted.

"This isn't over, Wilder," Travis said on his way out. "Dustin's right in there, Mr. Futterman."

Futterman stood glaring at me, the veins on his temples throbbing.

"This time you've really gone too far," he said, pointing a finger in my face. "Now don't give me a big song and dance. Just hand it over!"

"Hand what over, sir?"

"You know very well what I'm talking about," Futterman said in a low, intense voice. "Mrs. Platt said you've been hanging around the box office all night – and that you were there just now, creating a diversion, when the money disappeared."

Suddenly that conversation between Jeremy and Travis I'd overheard was making sense. My mind was trying to piece all the facts together so I could save my own hide.

"I didn't take it!" I said. "But I think I know where the money might be."

"Well?"

"In that stall with Jeremy."

"Oh, give me a break," Jeremy said from inside the stall. "He's lying like a rug."

"Open the door and prove me wrong."

Futterman knocked on the stall door. "Come on out, Mr. Wilder."

"I'm changing," Jeremy snapped. "I've got an interview to do any minute."

"Open that door right now!" Futterman demanded.

There was a pause. Then the stall door jiggled – and jiggled some more.

"I can't," Jeremy said, rattling the door. "It's stuck!"

"*Not again!*" Futterman and I both shouted.

"I've been meaning to get that thing fixed," Futterman said.

As if things weren't crazy enough, the director from *Show-Biz Beat* exploded into the bathroom, looking frazzled.

"Is Jeremy Jason Wilder here?" he asked. "Some lady in a turban told us he might be."

"I'm here!" Jeremy said.

"Great!" The director opened the bathroom door and yelled into the hall, "Let's set up!"

"In the can?" the cameraman asked, peeking inside.

"We don't have a choice," the director said, waving the whole crew in. "We're on a super-tight schedule. C'mon, people! Chop-chop!"

The techies rushed around, unrolling cables, plugging in cords, and setting up equipment. Callie Sinclair floated in, still going over her notes, while the makeup lady trailed her, brushing white flecks off her collar.

"Give me lights!" the director yelled. A sunburst filled the bathroom.

"Is anybody listening?" Jeremy shouted, rattling the door. *"I'm stuck in the stall!"*

"Not a problem," one of the techies said. He pulled a power screwdriver from his canvas bag and unscrewed the hinges on the stall door faster than Callie could take a swig from her bottled water. Jeremy was still in his street clothes, slumped on the toilet seat with both hands shielding his eyes from the blinding light.

"Well, it's not pretty," the cameraman said, looking through his camera lens, "but we'll have to make do."

"I like it," the director said. "It's raw, it's gritty – it's real life. Ready, Cal?"

"Let's do it!" she answered with a toss of her strawberry blond mane, and stood next to Jeremy.

"Are you guys crazy?" he said. "I'm not doing an interview on a –"

"Okay, people," the director interrupted, "in five, four –"

"Wait, shoot me from my left," Jeremy said. "That's my good side."

"– three, two –" The director pointed at Callie.

"Callie Sinclair here at Buttermilk Falls Elementary – in the boys' bathroom of all places – with *Double Take* star Jeremy Jason Wilder."

He flashed a smile, looking instantly cool and calm.

"Jeremy, you were suffering from a tarnished reputation after your sitcom was canceled. Now you're doing a school fund-raiser. Quite a transformation. Tell us a little about what led up to this night."

The director motioned for Jeremy to stand up, but he wouldn't. Callie lowered the microphone under his chin.

"There's not much to tell, really," Jeremy said. "The school needed me to raise money. They asked me to do the play as a favor, and I was happy to do it. No big deal."

Futterman grunted and folded his arms.

"But it *is* a big deal," Callie said. "Now, tell us about your leg injury."

"What? This?" Jeremy said, pulling up his pant leg to

uncover a thick bandage. "A fluke accident. I really don't wanna get into it."

"Please," Callie insisted.

"Well, let's just say there was a small child, a softball, and a speeding bus. I was there in the nick of time, yada yada yada."

What?

"So modest. You're a hero!" Callie squeezed his shoulder.

"Pan in, Archie," the director instructed the cameraman. "Tighter."

I couldn't stand there listening to Jeremy's lies without saying anything.

"Pssst. Excuse me, Miss Sinclair?" I whispered, inching closer to her. "Ask the modest hero about the stolen box-office money."

"The what?" Callie said out of the corner of her rigid smile.

"The money from the box office that he just ripped off."

"Hey, kid, get out of the shot!" the director snarled. "Cut! Cut!"

"No, keep rolling," Callie said. "This could be interesting."

The director threw up his hands, but I noticed that the little light on the front of the camera never went out. It suddenly hit me that I was on a national television program that would be aired in front of millions of people. I wasn't even that nervous.

"That's quite a serious accusation," Callie said directly into the camera. "It looks like it's coming from one of your fellow cast members, Jeremy." She shifted her attention to me. "Your name?"

"Dustin Grubbs," I said into the microphone. "With two *b*'s."

"And who do you play?"

"The Prince. Well, I originally had the Jester role, but Jeremy stole that too."

"He's wacko!" Jeremy yelled. "I've never seen this kid before in my life."

"Hello! I'm wearing a costume! He's lying, like he lied about everything else."

"What are you saying?" Callie said.

"He really *did* hurt his leg, but it was because he was showing off in gym class," I said. "Plus, I saw him tearing down the hall just a few minutes ago, so how bad could it be? I mean, come on."

"And he didn't exactly jump at the chance to take part in the play," Futterman said, stepping forward.

"And you are?" Callie held the microphone up to Futterman, who squashed in between us.

"Dan Futterman. Am I on TV?"

"Yes."

"I'm the principal here at Buttermilk Falls Elementary. Go, Fireballs!"

"Oh, no," Jeremy said, covering his face with his hands.

"Principal Futterman, please continue."

"Well, when we received Jeremy's test scores from

California, we found out he was reading at a fourth-grade level. His teacher, Miss Honeywell, graciously agreed to provide him with some private tutoring so he could advance to the seventh grade next year. I asked him if he wouldn't mind returning the favor by helping us out with the play."

"Bribed me is more like it," Jeremy muttered.

"Fourth-grade reading level? Really?" I said, turning to him. "Spell *orangutan*."

"Shove it!"

"But what's this about stolen money?" Callie asked me.

"From what I can tell, Jeremy must've borrowed some money from this evil rich kid named Travis Buttrick," I said. "I guess he couldn't pay it back. I'm not sure why –"

"I'm a TV star," Jeremy interrupted. "I don't have to borrow money."

"Wait!" I said, thinking back to the day we introduced ourselves in the cafeteria. "First you told us that all your money was tied up in some special account that you can't touch till you're, like, eighteen. Then you started showing up at school with a bunch of expensive new stuff." I looked directly into the camera lens. "America, you do the math."

"Pan in on the dorky kid in tights," the director instructed.

"Hey, I'm the one being interviewed," Jeremy said, grabbing the microphone away from me. I grabbed it right back.

"Travis must've talked him into ripping off the box office

to pay him back," I said, piecing it together in my head. "I'm no Sherlock Holmes, but according to my calculations, the money should be here in this stall."

"This interview is over!" Jeremy shouted. "Cut! Cut!"

"You can't say cut," the director said. "Only the director says cut."

Futterman unzipped the garment bag hanging on the stall door and searched inside. "No cash in here," he said, looking puzzled.

Jeremy was fuming. "I'm not going to sit here and take this!"

"Then stand up," I told him. "Show us what you're hiding in that toilet."

"Oh, do you really think that's such a good idea?" Callie asked, cringing.

"Are you kidding? This is pure gold," the director said, motioning to the cameraman. "Get a tight shot of the bowl, Archie."

"Wilder, whatever you do, don't flush!" Futterman warned. *"Do not flush!"*

Just then there were running footsteps, and LMNOP burst into the bathroom.

"Where's Dustin Grubbs?" she said, panting.

"Hold it down, little girl," a techie said, grabbing her arm. "We're rolling!"

"I don't care, this is important," LMNOP said, breaking

away. "Dustin Grubbs, your whole family just ran out of the auditorium!"

"Why?" I asked. "What happened?" *Maybe Dad showed up!*

"I'm not sure. Something about rushing your grandma to the emergency room!"

Chapter 19

A Chip Off the Ol' Tortilla Chip

"Omigod, I heard!" Wally said when I passed him in the hall. "You can take my bike to the hospital – it's chained to the fence. Come on, I'll show you."

That's the thing about best friends. You snap right out of hating each other's guts in the face of an emergency.

"Where do you think you two are going?" Futterman called after us. We didn't answer. "You'd better be back at seven-thirty – at the latest!"

I threw myself through the main doors and out into the night. The jolt of cool air made me feel as if I were stepping into another world. Wally and I jogged past the crammed parking lot to the fence where his bike stood.

"Come on, come on. . . ." Wally was talking to the lock, or the key, or himself. "Oh, crud, it broke!"

"What? The key?"

"It cracked right in half," he said, throwing the pieces into a bush.

"This is a nightmare! What am I supposed to do now?"

"Calm down," Wally said, looking around. "We need somebody with a car."

"Okay, let's jet!"

We tore down the sidewalk, back toward school. Wally was running faster than I'd ever seen him move in my life. The sight of his fake beard blowing in the breeze would've cracked me up if I weren't freaking out about Granny.

"Don't worry," he said, looking as worried as I was. "I'm sure she's just fine."

I knew right then and there what *real* friendship was. And I promised myself that I'd try my best not to screw it up again.

The tall auditorium windows were glowing orange, and I could see the silhouettes of audience members already filing in, like eager shadow puppets. I wondered if Dad was one of them, and how upset he'd be after coming all the way from Chicago for nothing. Futterman would eventually have to make a speech: "Ladies and gentlemen, due to unforeseen circumstances tonight's show has been canceled. We'd be happy to refund your money, but unfortunately, it's gone down the toilet along with Dustin Grubbs's hopes and dreams. Thank you for coming, and drive safely."

Truth is, I didn't give a rat's behind about the play anymore – I just wanted my gran to be okay. She was the oldest person I knew. "I'm not long for this world," she'd always say, especially when her arthritis flared up. They were just words that everyone brushed away – until now.

"Miss Van Rye!" Wally shouted. She looked like a mountain of glitter in front of the school's main entrance. "Could you drive Dustin to the hospital?"

"Oh, my stars," she said. "What happened? Dustin, are you all right?"

We filled her in, and she grabbed my hand, leading me down the sidewalk.

"My car is buried in the lot, but my date just arrived. He's looking for a spot on Spruce." Miss Van Rye looked up and down the street, twisting her pearl necklace.

"Here he is!" she shouted. She flagged down a sporty red car that screeched to a stop next to the curb. "I can't leave the rest of the cast high and dry, Dustin. But my date'll get you to the hospital in two shakes!"

"Thanks," I said.

She whispered something to the man behind the wheel and ushered me into the backseat. Wally stood on the school steps, giving me the thumbs-up.

"Don't you worry," Miss Van Rye said, slamming the car door. "I'm sure your grandma is just fine."

Why is everyone saying that? People aren't rushed to the hospital when they're just fine.

The next ten minutes were a blur of worry and trees whooshing by. But when we got to Buttermilk Falls Memorial Hospital and I saw Miss Van Rye's date get out of the car, I honestly thought I was going to have to check myself in.

"Maybe I should wait here," he said as we entered the bright lobby. "Your mom's probably upset enough already, and it could get sticky trying to explain . . . you know."

It was Mr. Ortega. Doughnut-stuffing, toupee-wearing, mother-dumping Mr. Ortega. I hadn't seen hide nor synthetic hair of him since our elegant dinner for four.

"That's probably a good idea," I said. If Mom knew what was going on, she'd have to check herself in too. Maybe we could get a group discount.

"The reception area is right over there," Mr. Ortega said, pointing to a long marble desk. "That nurse'll tell you where your grandma is."

The nurse gave me a plastic pass with a big red *E* on it and told me how to get to the emergency wing. She was nice enough, but she had a strange look on her face, as if she was holding something back. *Granny Grubbs is dead and she can't spit it out.* I nodded and said "thank you," but I wasn't paying attention to her directions and ended up getting lost in the endless puke green halls.

The water balloons in my stomach were back, and sloshier than ever. The smell of disinfectant stinking up the place didn't help. Neither did the signs: *Hazardous Hospital Waste!*

Quarantine! Airborne Infectious Disease! Morgue This Way. I ran in the opposite direction, holding my breath.

The maze of tiled hallways was leading me right back to where I'd started. An old woman in a wheelchair rolled by and I thought for a second that it was Granny. But her hair was too long – and too blue. I turned another corner to a strong whiff of coffee. Vending machines. And where there was food, could the Grubbs family be far away?

"Dustin! What are you doing here?"

It was Aunt Birdie! She was sitting next to Aunt Olive, who was sitting across from –

"Mom!"

I ran to her and smothered her with a hug. The next thing I knew I was bawling – buckets! Everything came gushing out of me, like an open fire hydrant on a ninety-degree day.

"She's okay," Mom said, stroking my hair. "Granny's just fine."

There's that "just fine" again. I didn't want to let go of Mom. My body started doing that weird heaving thing where you can't catch your breath after crying too hard.

"Are you sure?" I asked, pulling back to look into her eyes for an honest answer. "I can take the truth." Oh, who was I kidding? I could take the truth only if it was good news, not bad.

"That *is* the truth," Mom said, handing me a tissue.

"Well, what happened?"

"Why don't you ask her yourself?"

I turned to see Granny and a man in a white coat walking toward us. I rushed to her and wrapped my arms around her middle.

"Oh, look!" Granny said. "A handsome prince has come to rescue me! Where'd you park your horse?"

I looked down at myself and saw a gold tunic and white tights. No wonder people were staring. I'd forgotten that I was wearing my costume – well, Felix's costume.

"This is my grandson Dustin," Granny said, introducing me to the doctor. "He doesn't always dress like this."

"Dr. Devon," the man said, shaking my hand.

"What was wrong, Doctor?" I asked. Then I realized that Granny had on an eye patch under her glasses, over her left eye.

"Corneal abrasion," Dr. Devon said.

I gave him a puzzled look. It sounded serious.

"A minor scratch on her eyeball," he explained. "The patch will do the trick."

"Now all I need is a peg leg and a parrot," Granny said.

"You do look like Pirate Pete from the Crustacean Crunch commercials. How the heck did it happen?"

"It was the darnedest thing," she said. "We were at your school for the play, and your aunt Birdie gave me some tortilla chips – what are they called? Corn Fritters or some such thing. Not Corn Fritters. Burritos? Lolitas?"

"Cornchitas?" I said.

"No, no, no. Those spicy triangles. Oh, you know what I'm talking about," Granny said. "Cornchitas, that's it!"

The doctor gave me a quick wink.

"Anyway, I took a bite and the tip of a chip broke off and flew right into my eye."

"Oh, cripes!"

"Stung like the dickens," she said. "They were the barbecue kind, so that made it even worse. No, not barbecue – cheddar cheese and onion. No – jalapeño!"

As a kid with firsthand experience of spaghetti sauce up the nose, I could relate.

"Well, I'm glad you're all right," I said, giving her another hug.

"Look at the two of us," Granny said. "The prince and the pirate. We might as well go trick-or-treating."

With a "yo-ho-ho and a bottle of rum," we made our way to the orange vinyl chairs, where the rest of the family was sitting and drinking tea. Dr. Devon explained the details of Granny's injury to the family and told us how the eyeball was one of the fastest-healing parts of the body. The Grubbs women were staring him down as if he'd stepped off the cover of *Dream Doctor* magazine.

"We appreciate everything you've done, Doctor," Mom said, extending her hand.

"My pleasure," Dr. Devon said, taking her hand in both of his.

I swear Mom was blushing. It made me squirm to see her acting like Darlene does around Jeremy.

The doctor gave Granny her instructions, making sure we all heard. "Leave the patch on for a full three days," he said. "You can take two acetaminophen every four hours if there's any pain. If you sit tight, I can have the pharmacy send up your drops."

"Thanks, Doc," Granny said.

"And I'll see you back here on Monday for a follow-up. All right, young lady?"

"It's a date!"

"Nice meeting all of you," Dr. Devon said, flashing his hundred-watt smile.

"He's a real looker, that one," Granny said, watching him walk away. "And no wedding ring. If only I were twenty years younger."

"Twenty?" Aunt Olive said.

"If ifs and buts were candy and nuts we'd all have a wonderful Christmas," Aunt Birdie said, ripping into a snack bag. "Here, Ma, have some of these – they're dee-lish."

"Cornchitas?" Granny said. "I swear, Birdie, sometimes I think the elevator's not reaching your top floor."

"Dr. Julius Devon," Aunt Olive sang his name. "It's like music."

"How long do you think that prescription'll take?" I asked. "'Cause we should be heading back to the school." It was as if I were invisible.

"What a catch, Dorothy!" Gran said, nudging Mom. "I wonder if he knows you're available. Shoot, even with one eye I saw sparks between the two of you."

"Oh, please," Mom muttered.

"Did you notice his eyes?" Aunt Birdie said. "A perfect shade of sea-foam blue."

"Sea foam is green," I said. "And we really should go."

"I'm telling you, Dorothy, you have to strike while the iron's hot," Granny said. "You're not getting any younger, you know."

"Okay, that's it," Mom said, getting up. "I'm going to wait in the car."

"That's a start!" I said.

"I don't understand you sometimes," Granny said, pulling her back. "A handsome doctor's not good enough? After my good-for-nothing son runs off and deserts you, you lock yourself in the house for three years. Then all of a sudden you're gaga over that rumpled doughnut salesman. That Larry, or Gary, or –"

"Barry?" Mom said.

"No, that's not it," Granny said.

Mr. Ortega's head popped up from the water fountain.

"Barry, what are you doing here?" Mom said, falling back into her chair.

"Oh! Hello, Dot – Dorothy," Mr. Ortega said, all wide eyed. "Uh, I drove Dustin. Didn't he tell you?"

"No."

"It slipped my mind," I said.

"I was going to the school play and Regina said your son needed a ride, so –"

"Regina?" Mom interrupted.

Mr. Ortega just stood there, stone-faced and silent, like Felix Plunket when he'd freaked out onstage. Then he suddenly crouched down next to Granny and shouted, "Are you all right, Mother Grubbs?" as if she were deaf.

"Keep your voice down – you're in a hospital," Granny said, hoisting herself out of her seat. "I think I forgot my pocketbook in Dr. Divine's office."

"Your purse is right there," Mom said, pointing to it. "And it's Devon."

"Then I forgot to ask him something," Granny said, shooting Mom an annoyed look. "I'll be right back."

"I'll phone Regina and tell her everything is fine and dandy, and that Dustin's on his way," Mr. Ortega said nervously. He wandered over to a vending machine, dropped some coins in, and wrestled out a candy bar. "Okeydokey, then. I guess I'll see you folks at the play."

Everyone muttered an anemic good-bye. Mr. O. left, and my aunts went to "powder their noses" in the ladies' room.

"Who's this Regina?" Mom asked after we were alone.

"Miss Van Rye, the kindergarten teacher," I said. "She helped with the play."

"Well, that explains a lot."

"So where's Turdface?" I asked, changing the subject.

"Your brother doesn't even know we're here," Mom said. "He's meeting us at the play with his new girlfriend."

"Oh, no! And you're letting him? This one could be, like, a vampire or a stripper or something."

Mom gave me her oh-you're-overreacting-again look and took a sip of tea.

"He really seems to like this girl," she said, smiling. "And no tattoos!"

"You know who else might be meeting us at the play?" I blurted out.

She'd find out soon enough if he showed up; I figured I'd give her fair warning. And if *she* overreacted – well, the emergency room was just steps away.

"Who?"

I couldn't say it. Then I thought about how she didn't even flinch when Gordy told her I wanted to be an actor. This was a lot different, though, and I knew it. I took a deep breath and said it on the exhale.

"Dad."

Mom's face went whiter than a hospital sheet.

"What?" she said, knocking over her tea. "But when did you – how did you –"

"I left him a message at a club he's working at in Chicago – I kinda tracked him down. Said I was doing a play and that maybe he'd want to come see it. Then he sent me a telegram at school, saying he was coming. Did you know that telegrams still exist?"

Mom didn't speak. She grabbed a bunch of napkins that were on the table, wadded them up, and started stabbing at the spill.

"Who put you up to this?" she finally said, still stabbing. "One of your aunts?"

"No, it was my idea. I never thought in a million years he'd say yes."

"Oh, Dustin. . . ." She looked at me as if I'd just murdered someone, as if I were standing over the body, dripping in blood. "And you waited until the last minute to spring this on me? What's your grandmother going to do when she sees him?" She sat quietly for a minute, just staring at the soaked napkins on the table. "I – I just don't think I can face that man again. What would I say?"

"Hello?"

"This isn't a joke, Dustin," Mom said sharply. Her face was clenched as tight as a fist. "How could you do such a thing?"

"Well, he *is* my father!"

She grabbed her jacket and purse and rushed into the hall, almost slamming into Aunt Olive, who was walking out of the ladies' room.

"Mom!" I called after her. A burly nurse shushed me. "Mom, wait!"

I instantly regretted telling her. Regretted everything.

"Where's she running off to?" Aunt Olive asked. "Did you tell her about –?"

Aunt Olive was the only person I'd talked to about Dad coming – well, until now.

"I had to," I mumbled. I should've been dehydrated from before, but I could taste the salty tears running over my lips. "I hope she doesn't take a bus home or something."

Aunt Birdie flew out of the ladies' room and migrated from side table to side table, hand-sweeping crumbs and picking up empty wrappers and cups.

"I thought Granny wasn't coming to the play," I whispered to Aunt Olive. "What's gonna happen if Dad shows up?"

"Well, I tried to get her to stay home," she said, rubbing my shoulder, "but you know your gran – she insisted on coming. Maybe now she –"

"What's all this whispering about?" Aunt Birdie said, dumping the trash into the receptacle next to us. "And where did they go for that prescription, Timbuktu? It's ten to eight. We should skedaddle."

My heart jumped. "We have to go!" I said, sniffling. "Now!"

"Here she comes," Aunt Olive said as Granny came shuffling around the corner. "She won't be up for your play after all this hoopla. I'll drop her off at home."

"Don't you dare," Granny said, joining us. "And I can speak for myself, Olive, thank you very much."

"You really should get some rest now," Aunt Birdie said, taking Granny's arm.

"I'll get plenty of rest when I'm six feet under."

"Oh, Ma, how you talk," Aunt Olive said. "We're only trying to –"

"Listen!" Granny growled in her drill-sergeant voice. "This child has his play to do. Can't you see he's on pins and needles? Now, I've got the prescription in my pocketbook, so stop your jabbering and let's vamoose!"

Chapter 20

Row C, Seat 101

"He's here!" Wally and Pepper both shouted when Aunt Olive's station wagon dropped me off in front of the school. They were in costume, jumping up and down in the entranceway. I had to climb over Mom, who hadn't said a word to anyone for the entire drive over and was still sizzling with anger – but at least she was there. The car sped off to find parking, and I sped up the steps.

"Come on, hustle!" Pepper said, pulling me into the corridor. Shouts of "He's here! He's here!" echoed off the walls. I felt important.

"We're holding the curtain," Wally said, "but the audience is getting antsy."

"They passed antsy ten minutes ago," Pepper said. "They're about to start throwing rotten fruit."

The three of us raced down the hall as if we were running

on hot coals. The muffled roar of the audience grew louder and louder the closer we got to the auditorium. My mind was a total mishmash from the night so far – and the main-event stuff hadn't even happened yet.

"I'm glad you're back," Wally said, "and that your grandma's okay. Miss Van Rye gave us the scoop."

"Here!" Pepper flung a garment bag at my head. "Get dressed, quick!"

"I *am* dressed."

"As the Prince," she said. "But you're back to playing the Jester again, 'cause Jeremy flew the coop!"

"No way!"

"Way!" Pepper said. "He cut out after Futterman said he would press charges."

"Yeah, but first he made Jeremy scoop the stolen box-office money out of the toilet," Wally said. "On national television! How cool is that?"

"I knew it was in the bowl!" I said.

"Futterman said celebrity or not, a thief is a thief," Pepper said, "and that there would be swift . . . revolution, or something."

"Persecution?" Wally said.

"No."

"Retribution?" I said.

"That's it!" Pepper said. "At least the idiot left his costume behind."

"Wait," I said. "If I'm playing the Jester, who's gonna be the Prince?"

"Felix," Wally said.

"Cynthia's helping him go over his lines in the kindergarten room right now," Pepper said. "Take off your costume and I'll bring it to him. It'll save time."

"But –"

"Take it off!" she insisted. "This is no time to be shy."

I undid my tie belt and handed it to Wally, then pulled off the gold tunic and tossed it to Pepper. There I was, running around half-naked in public again. *I really should start working out.*

Pepper hiked up her dress and zoomed down the hall, shouting, "See ya in Galico!"

"Felix Plunket?" I said to Wally. "How did they get ahold of him?"

"Futterman spotted him in the audience," he said. "I didn't think Felix would go for it, but he jumped at the chance. Said something about wanting a do-over."

The Walrus helped me on with Jeremy's Jester costume, the rental from Hollywood Costume Cavalcade. It was a zillion times better than my original, with red, green, and yellow satiny pieces all sewn together in a diamond pattern – and a huge zigzag collar with tiny bells attached to the tips.

I popped my head through the neck hole and saw Miss

Van Rye barreling toward us in her blinding sequins, her pearls rattling. Little reflections of light bounced off her and filled the hallway.

"Oh, thank goodness you're here!" Miss Van Rye said, suffocating me in a bear hug. "Switching back to Jingle Jangles shouldn't be a problem for you, trouper that you are. Felix may need some help, though. I'm counting on you to get him through this."

Okay, no pressure.

The backstage doors sprang open and Futterman's bald head poked through.

"You're here!" he said. "It's about time. Let's go!" The doors closed, then opened again, like a cuckoo clock. "Don't mess up this time!"

Pepper was leading the rest of the cast down the hall in a mad dash to the auditorium. It sounded like a stampede of water buffalo.

"Shhh, quiet as church mice," Miss Van Rye said in a hushed voice. She held the backstage door open and herded us onto the stage. "Break legs, munchkins. And just remember to have fun."

"Places, people!" Futterman yelled from the darkness.

It was lucky that the jester's hat Miss Honeywell had made for me was sitting on the prop table, 'cause Jeremy's came down over my eyes. Big head – go figure. Wally handed me my tie belt, and I quickly wrapped it around my waist, knotting it on the side. Now the costume felt complete.

I began pacing back and forth, going over the Jester lines in my head. It wasn't easy with the audience jabbering and clapping in rhythm.

"This must be what it felt like in medieval times," Wally said, "when they threw people to the lions."

"Roman times."

"Huh?"

"They threw people to the lions in – ouch!" I rammed into the prop table. My eyes were having a hard time adjusting to the dark.

"Are you all right?" Wally asked.

"Yes. No!" A surge of panic shot through me. "The audience is going to boo me off the stage!"

"Why?"

"They paid to see Jeremy Jason Wilder, not me!"

"So? You're a ten-times-better Jester."

I really needed that. Friends till the end.

The houselights went out. Everything got quiet.

"Wally?" I whispered, grabbing his arm with both hands. "My dad might be out in that audience right now."

"Your *real* dad?"

"No, the guy who plays my dad on TV. Of course, my real dad!"

The musical intro started playing through the speaker system, and Cynthia launched into her minstrel song onstage.

Many sunrises ago, in the Land of Galico,
On a warm and dewy, bright September morn,
There arose unbounded bliss, unimagined happiness,
For the daintiest of princesses was born. . . .

She sounded kind of wobbly on her last verse, but things just rolled along without a hitch after that. Leonard Shempski even got the sound cues right. Felix was sweating up a storm again, but the gods of theater must've been smiling down on us, 'cause he managed to get every word out this time – with hardly a stutter. I kept checking out seat C101, the one that was reserved for Dad. It stayed empty for all of act one.

Maybe he came late and he's standing at the back of the house. Or he might be just minutes away; trains never run on time. All my good stuff is in act two, anyway.

I spent the whole intermission peeking through that trusty hole in the curtain. It looked as though some of the audience had left, probably because psycho Jeremy wasn't in the play. I spotted Gordy and some girly-girl huddled together, reading programs. Aunt Birdie was sitting next to them, snapping a flash picture of Granny hiding behind her purse. Mom and Aunt Olive were standing by the covered piano, chatting with Pepper's folks. No sign of Dad.

Could it be that I just don't recognize him? I mean, it's been a while. People change. I tried to avoid the depressing maybe-he-just-blew-me-off thoughts that were knocking around in my brain. I still had to be funny for forty-five more minutes.

"Places for act two, kiddles!" Miss Van Rye shouted, racing across the stage like a streak of silver lightning.

Somewhere around the beginning of the second act, when I was onstage without many lines, I glanced out into the house at third-row center and just about freaked out. A dark silhouette was filling the aisle seat reserved for Mr. Theodore Grubbs. Adrenaline rush! Just knowing he was out there watching made my performance more energetic or something. I thought I'd been giving it my all, but I guess not, 'cause suddenly it felt as if I was running on high voltage.

"No, Father!" Pepper said, bursting into tears. "I cannot marry the Prince, for his heart beats cold. And truth be known, I love another – Jingle Jangles the Jester!"

"And I love her!" I said, leaping forward, feeling the love oozing out of every pore.

"Young fool," Wally said, chuckling. "Surely you jest?"

"I jest indeed – 'tis my lot in life. But I assure you, my love for your daughter is true."

"But you're nothing but a simpleton, a worthless twit, a penniless boor –"

"I get the point," I said with a deadpan look toward the audience. *Huge laugh. I'll probably be nominated for a Tony Award.*

"Simple, perhaps," I continued as the laugh died down, "yet my riches abound."

"Limericks and limber limbs are not the riches of which I speak!" Wally said.

"Nor I, Your Majesty."

I ran offstage and came back with a burlap sack, which I ripped open at Wally's feet. Shiny coins and jewels came spilling out, and the lords and ladies oohed and aahed.

"My dear father left this to me upon his untimely passing. It seems that over his lifetime as court jester, he'd collected a small fortune – as did his father before him and *his* father before *him*. A bauble for a bawdy verse, a fourpence for a ditty . . ."

"Oh, Jing!" Pepper gushed, wrapping her arms around me.

The cast cheered, and the audience did too.

"Well, well, it seems that true love and a frugal nature have conquered all," Wally said. "So raise your goblets high, good folk! Let the celebration commence!"

The curtain closed behind Cynthia and her lute, and she sang the closing song:

Thus ends our tale of crowns and clowns, and love so fair and true,
And in our wake I hope you'll take this thought away with you:

While breeding, grace, and handsome face are lovely to behold,
A titter here, a giggle there, are worth their weight in gold!

Curtain call. I was up last. Maybe it was just me, but I swear the applause-o-meter went crazy when I took my bow. *Actors are lucky. Not many people get applause. Even the guy who cloned that sheep probably just got a hearty handshake.* It was like being in a ticker-tape parade, jumping out of an airplane, and winning the lottery all at the same time. Like a thousand pats on the back saying, "Great job, Dustin Grubbs!"

The cast formed a line across the front of the stage for our final bow, and the audience gave us a standing ovation! I must've been hovering about three feet off the ground. The houselights came up and I got a good look at the first row. Mom, Granny – even Gordy and his new girlfriend were on their feet, clapping. My eyes shot over to third-row center – the aisle seat C101. Crash and burn.

Unless Dad had transformed into a tall black woman, he was a no-show.

Chapter 21

Most Valuable Player

"Fire up the grill, Ed!" Bunny hollered, holding open the door of the Yankee Doodle Diner. "Christmas just came early this year!"

The whole cast and half the audience piled into the diner, taking up every chair, stool, and booth for this unplanned celebration. Futterman, who was acting very un-Futtermanly, waved a fistful of wet money over his head and announced, "Order all the Uncle Sam Burgers and Doodle Dogs you want, folks. It's taken care of!"

"Eat your heart out, Jukebox Café!" Bunny shouted to her competition across the street.

It was the best night of my life and the worst. It's hard being both happy and miserable at the same time, and I wasn't going to eenie-meenie-miney-mo. So I opted for miserable.

Aunt Olive had dropped Mom and me off at the diner and driven Granny and Aunt Birdie home. I wanted to go home too, but Mom thought it'd be a good idea if we put in an appearance, since I was the star and everything. She was in a much better mood, probably 'cause Dad never showed up. We squeezed into a booth with Wally and his parents. They'd be driving us home. I didn't feel much like eating – or breathing.

"I'm sorry he disappointed you," Mom whispered.

Or talking.

"I know you were hoping for a happy ending, like in the play," she went on, "but that doesn't always happen in real life."

The Dorkins were gushing about Wally's performance and asking him stuff like, "How did you remember all those lines?" So they weren't listening in, I don't think.

"He's always marched to a different drummer, your father," Mom said, straightening her silverware. Mrs. Sternhagen used to say that about me too, but I thought it was a good thing. "Maybe I'm too overprotective of you and Gordy when it comes to him," she said, "but I know how it hurts when someone you care about doesn't live up to your expectations."

"Yeah. Now I know what a bowling pin feels like."

The smell of fresh peach pie came wafting by – but it wasn't on the menu. It turned out to be Miss Honeywell. She floated up to our booth, wearing a silky dress splattered with pink rosebuds. *Why is the town's deputy sheriff standing in her shadow?*

"Dustin, I'm just so gosh-darn proud of you," she said. "The audience ate you up! Wonderful to see you again, Mrs. Grubbs. You have a very talented, enthusiastic son."

"Don't I know it!"

"And what a fine job you did too, Wallace."

Miss Honeywell finally noticed that King Kong was breathing down her neck.

"Oh, where are my manners?" she said. "I'm sure y'all know my fiancé, Mr. Lutz, the deputy sheriff."

"Fiancé"? She's engaged to that science experiment gone wrong?

The adults at the table congratulated them, and Lutz the Klutz grunted. He had Olympic-size sweat pools around his pits. Miss Honeywell was blushing, and she grabbed his hairy hand, all lovey-dovey. Well, if it had to happen, I'm glad it was near the end of the school year. I don't think I could've lived through seeing her in class every day, knowing she belonged to another man – and one who was allowed to carry firearms.

Okay, can we please get through the rest of the night without any more surprises?

I sank low into the cracked vinyl, trying to make out the words that were bleeding through a flyer taped to the window: TRECNOC GNIRPS. I was thinking of what Mom said. It really does sting like hot arrows when somebody lets you down.

"Spring concert," I said out loud.

"Huh?" Wally said.

"The flyer – on the window right behind you. Check it out."

Wally reached around, peeled the flyer off the window, and gave it the once-over.

"It says there's an outdoor concert in Lotustown. It's next Saturday."

"Cool," I said. "Wanna go? My treat."

"It's free."

"Like I said, my treat."

"But it's classical," Wally said, scrunching up his face. "You *hate* classical music."

"Yeah? So?"

Wally stared at me as if he were counting pores. I figured it was about time I bit the bullet and did something that he liked to do, for a change. People could slip right through your fingers if you didn't hang on tight enough.

"Okay," he said. His eyes were shining brighter than Miss Van Rye's sequined dress. "Let's go!"

"You're on – Wallace."

Bunny zoomed over to our table and took our drink order. She brought us our two Diet Cokes and three regulars in record time. The booth was rattling with conversation, but my mind kept jumping back to one thing. It wasn't long before my thoughts turned into words.

"There could be, like, a *million* reasons why Dad didn't come," I said to Mom. "What if he's really sick – or hurt? What then?"

"Dustin, for heaven's sake," Mom said out of the side of her mouth, "just drop it, okay?" She took a long sip of Coke through her straw and swallowed hard. "He didn't have much of a problem dropping *us*."

"That's not true," I blurted out. "He used to call the house, and you kept it a big secret from me and Gordy. And I know he used to send us presents too, but you sent them right back."

I knew I was sworn to secrecy, and I didn't want to upset her twice in one night, but the words just came out. Mom had that surprised look on her face again. Shocked, even. But I could tell from her reaction that what I had said was true.

"I'm really fed up with your aunts' filling your head with this garbage!"

"But it's *not* garbage, is it?"

No answer. Wally's family stopped talking. They were probably listening to every word we were saying. I didn't care.

"I mean, what's the big deal if I talk to Dad every once in a while? Or see him, even?"

"Dustin, I can't believe you're thinking of such things after what he pulled tonight. When will you learn? Enough is enough!"

"You're a Grand Old Flag" came blaring through the diner's

new jukebox, and that was the end of that. *It was hard to admit, but Mom was right. He had his chance and he blew it.*

The chitchat in the booth slowly picked up again. I dug into my pocket and pulled out the *Reach for the Stars!* key chain Dad had given me. "To Dusty. Luv, Da." *That's how sixth-graders sign their Valentine's Day cards. "Luv" – not "love." 'Cause they don't really mean it.*

A spider plant was sitting on a ledge next to our booth. I reached over and dropped the key chain in the dirt.

"Attention, everybody," Futterman shouted. "Can I have everyone's attention, please?" He was standing on a chair, clinking his root-beer mug with a spoon.

Uh-oh. Now what?

"First off, great show!" he said as the talking petered out. "And we didn't need that smart-aleck Hollywood delinquent to pull it off either. Well, after all the tickets were sold, any-way." He chuckled at that. "The play tonight raised enough money to cover the repairs for the baby-grand piano – and then some! Who knew that people around here would go for this stuff in such a big way?"

"Hey!" Pepper's stepdad said with a mouthful of Doodle Dog. "Us Buttermilk Fallians appreciate culture too, ya know!"

"That's right," Mrs. Plunket said. "We're not a bunch of boobs and rubes."

"Okay, settle down," Futterman said, raising his voice over

the commotion. "I have more good news. First thing Monday morning I'm placing an order for the Mascot 2000 electronic scoreboard for our gymnasium! Plus, I think I could manage to set aside a little cash for next year's show."

"Next year's show"? I have to be dreaming. I'll be hitting that snooze button again any second now.

"Can we do a musical?" Darlene asked. "I've had three years of tap and baton."

"We'll see," Futterman said. "Now, I'm not real big on mushy sentiment, but I like to give credit where credit is due."

Since when? What's gotten into Futterman?

"Here's to everyone who made this night possible," he said, raising his mug. "Miss Van Rye, Miss Honeywell . . . and Dustin Grubbs, our MVP!"

Camera flashes went off in my face. Major head rush. My scalp was tingling.

"So, raise your goblets high, good folk!" Wally shouted. "To Dustin Grubbs – the biggest star *ever* to hit Buttermilk Falls!"

Well, I've never used the word *flabbergasted* before, but I was totally flabbergasted – especially when Felix told me what *MVP* stood for.

Chapter 22

That's a Wrap!

"Could somebody get the door?" Aunt Birdie called from the bathroom. "I'm not presentable."

"I'm on the phone!" I said with my hand covering the receiver. "Sorry, Dr. Devon. Yeah, Granny's just fine. Uh-huh. My mom? I think she's swamped in our kitchen right now, upstairs. Can you call back in, like, a half hour? Okay, nice speaking to you again too. Bye."

The doorbell rang three times in a row.

"Is someone gonna get that?" Granny hollered from her bedroom. "Or are you waiting for an engraved invitation?"

"I've got it, Gran!" I yelled.

Jeez, I officially live upstairs. How do they cope when I'm not here?

I opened the door and saw Aunt Olive's rear end. She was bent over, digging through her purse and mumbling. LMNOP was next to her, sitting on a stack of newspapers.

"Oh, thank goodness," my aunt said, looking frazzled. "I must've forgotten my keys. But look what the cat dragged in."

"Hi, Dustin Grubbs," LMNOP said.

"Hi."

I hadn't spoken to her since that day with the posters when I chewed her out. Not one of my best moments. I knew I owed her an apology for acting like a gigantic goober, but steering clear of her was a lot easier.

"I was just going to leave these papers on your porch, but then your aunt came and – well, anyway, you're in print again!" LMNOP said, flipping through one of the newspapers. "Page eight. Two whole paragraphs."

She handed me a copy of the *Penny Pincher,* a free local paper containing mostly grocery coupons and advertisements –

LOCAL BOY SAVES SHOW!

– and fascinating articles! My name had already appeared in bold type in last Sunday's *Willowbridge Gazette.* I wasn't letting it go to my head or anything, but in the week since the play I'd been treated like a celebrity in Buttermilk Falls. I was glad I had Jeremy Jason Wilder as a role model – of how *not* to behave.

"In or out?" Granny said, sneaking up behind me. "You're letting mosquitoes in the house."

"This is so excellent!" I said, skimming the article.

"Well, aren't you going to invite your little friend in,

Dustin?" Aunt Olive said, hanging her jacket on the coat stand. "After she went through so much trouble for you?"

"Sure, come on," I said. LMNOP followed us inside. "Our channel five upstairs is all fuzzy, so we're watching *Show-Biz Beat* down here. They're doing a follow-up on *Whatever Happened to My Favorite Celebrity Kids?* and Jeremy might be on."

Aunt Birdie hurried out of the bathroom with gigantic curlers in her hair and a green face. "Did I miss the program?" she asked.

"Alien abduction!" I yelled, diving onto the sofa. "Hide your organs!"

"Don't make me laugh," Aunt Birdie said, patting her face. "I'll crack!"

Everybody found a seat, and I read the article out loud. It mainly talked about the huge turnout we had for the show and how I'd switched roles at the last minute. Then it said, "The adroit Mr. Grubbs reveled in delightful antics as the Jester, skillfully providing comic relief." Aunt Olive said *adroit* was a good thing, that it meant I knew what I was doing.

"You're a hit!" Aunt Birdie said, and Granny kissed me on the head.

"Dustin's not the only big shot around here," Aunt Olive said. "Turns out Ellen's got a serious case of the smarts. Won second place in the National Science Fair. Show them your ribbon, honey."

LMNOP took off her backpack and spun it around. A yellow ribbon with shiny gold writing was pinned next to her *I'm Terrific!* button.

"All this time we had a genius living next door," Granny said, examining the ribbon. "Who'd have guessed?"

Not me, that's for sure.

"Well, aren't you going to congratulate her?" Aunt Olive said to me.

"Congratulations," I muttered. "What was your project on?"

"Oh, you don't want to know," LMNOP said.

I would've left it at that, but my aunts egged her on.

"Okay. It started out as a basic soil characterization study," she said, poking up her glasses. "I took sand, silt, and clay samples from all over Buttermilk Falls. Then I set up rain gauges and wind vanes, and measured pH levels so I could evaluate the harmful effects caused by acid rain. Oh, I'm boring you guys. I can tell."

The whole room was staring at her as if she were speaking in Japanese.

"No, go ahead, sweetie," Granny said. "We're listening."

"Well, that's it, really," LMNOP said, winding down. "I wanted to expand my research to the effect of acid rain on the aquatic ecosystem, but there wasn't enough time. There's always next year."

And all the while I thought she was making mud pies and burying doll parts.

"That's wonderful, Ellen," Aunt Olive said. "You keep at it and you'll go far."

"It's six o'clock," I said, clicking on the TV with the remote. "The show's on."

"What do they put in these facial masks anyway?" Aunt Birdie said with stiff lips. "Cement?"

"That looks like French clay," LMNOP said, studying her. "Montmorillonite."

"Oh, uh-huh," Aunt Birdie said. "You should try some, Ma. It's supposed to make your skin as smooth as a baby's bottom."

"You stay away from me with that stuff."

"Shhhh, it's on!" I said, turning up the volume.

Jeremy's face flashed on the TV screen. He and Callie Sinclair were sitting across from each other in brown leather chairs – definitely a step up from his last interview. We caught the tail end of Callie's question.

". . . a far cry from doing school plays and living at the Dew Drop Inn on the outskirts of Buttermilk Falls. What's it feel like to be back in Hollywood?"

"The Dew Drop Inn?" Aunt Birdie muttered. "That place is a dump."

"Shush!" Granny swatted her.

"It's great, Cal," Jeremy said. "With the *Double Take* lawsuits and stuff, my family was going through a pretty rough time moneywise, so we moved to Buttermilk Falls. It was a lot cheaper to live out in the middle of nowhere."

They were broke?

"Plus, my parents thought it'd be the best thing for me – and them. But they were wrong."

"I understand they're going through a divorce now," Callie said with a sorrowful head tilt. "That must be tough on you, huh?"

Looks like we had a lot more in common than I thought. Jeremy didn't answer, but ran his hands through his hair. He had a lump-in-your-throat look on his face.

"On an up note," Callie said in a cheerier voice, "I hear that the school has dropped the charges for that whole box-office mishap. Now it seems your bad-boy image has turned out to be a real career booster."

"Unreal, right? Yeah, I just signed on to play the son of a Mafia hit man in Francis Capelli's fall movie project."

"Quite a comeback! Before we go, is there anything you'd like to say to your friends back in Buttermilk Falls?"

"Nothing I can say on TV."

"There must be somebody you'd like to give a shout-out to."

"Well, there is one guy. We started out as pretty good friends, but things got screwed up in the end."

"Okay," Callie Sinclair said, "look right into that camera."

The camera panned in on Jeremy.

"We should be taping this," I said, leaning forward.

"Yo, Travis," Jeremy said, making a weird hand signal. "Hang tough, dude."

I grabbed the remote and clicked off the television.

"Well, wasn't that a slap in the face?" Aunt Olive said, opening the *Penny Pincher*.

That's just what it felt like. But what did I expect?

"Is it over already?" Granny asked, struggling to get off the couch. Aunt Birdie helped her, and they both headed toward the bathroom. "That boy on the TV looked familiar."

"It figures," LMNOP said to me. "I always knew they were in cahoots."

Cahoots? I stared at her, blinking my way back in time.

"So, *you* left me that note. How'd you get into the boys' locker room, anyway?"

"Easy. The janitor leaves the door wide open when he's mopping up on Fridays."

"And did you plant that tabloid article in my script too?"

"Guilty," LMNOP said. "I kept seeing Travis and Jeremy hanging out together, and I knew they were up to no good. You were furious with me, so –"

"Sorry about that whole thing," I mumbled. "I was mad about something else and took it out on you."

It actually felt good to finally say the *S*-word. It's kind of like trapped gas. You can live with it for so long, but then, when it finally belches its way free – relief!

"Oh, well," LMNOP said, grinning. "Everything turned out okay."

"All's well that end's well," Aunt Olive said. "That's Shakespeare, isn't it?"

Mom came trotting into the room, carrying a covered dish, with Gordy right behind. At least, it was someone who looked like Gordy. He was wearing a navy blue blazer, a clean white shirt, and a tie. His hair was combed, his shoes were shined – and I think he was wearing cologne.

"Now, this is the Gordy that does me proud," Mom said, setting her dish on the dining-room table. "I couldn't let him leave without showing him off first."

Mom was in a much better mood ever since she and Aunt Olive had cleared the air. I wasn't supposed to be listening, but my aunt basically apologized for telling me stuff about Dad behind her back. I was still glad she had, though.

"Very debonair!" Aunt Olive remarked. "What's the occasion?"

"No big deal. Just a date," Gordy said, futzing with his tie. "With Rebecca."

Rebecca was his latest girlfriend. Miss May. Totally different from the others, though. A freshman in college majoring in art history. Who knew what she saw in Scuzz-o? Opposites attract, I guess – just like Miss Honeywell and that lunkhead of a deputy sheriff. That's the only explanation that makes sense.

"So, where are the two of you off to, Mr. Fancy Pants?" Aunt Olive asked.

"The Willowbridge Opera," he said. "We're seeing something called *Carmen*."

Wait until he finds out it's not a show about auto mechanics.

"That's where I sang in my youth!" Aunt Olive cried out. "When it was just a fledgling company. *Carmen*, my favorite. Oh, the 'Habanera!'" She la-la-la'ed around the room, clicking her fingers as if they were castanets.

"Hey, Freakshow," Gordy said to me over Aunt Olive's singing. "Rebecca can't shut up about your stupid play. She's dying to meet you."

"Really?" I said. *I knew that girl had good taste.* "Perhaps I can pencil her in to my busy schedule. But somebody's gonna have to start kissing some major butt around here."

"Yeah, dream on."

Aunt Olive hit a high note and twirled into her armchair. "I just adore Bizet!"

"Oh, that was you, Olive?" Granny said, shuffling into the room with a scrubbed-faced Aunt Birdie at her heels. "I thought the smoke alarm went off. And who is that handsome young man?"

"That's Gordy, Ma," Aunt Birdie said slowly. "Your graaandson."

"I realize that, Birdie!" Granny snapped. "I wasn't having a senior moment, you know."

Gordy checked out his teeth in the hallway mirror, squeezed something on his chin, then headed out the door.

"Have a good evening, ladies," he said. I thought he was including me in that, but he added, "Later, dweeb."

"Bye, sludgeface," I said.

That was probably the warmest, fuzziest conversation we'd ever had. I owed a lot to Rebecca. Heck, the world owed a lot to Rebecca.

"Very spiffy," Aunt Birdie said, peeking through the blinds. "The new Gordy certainly is a breath of fresh air."

"True," I said. "He actually started showering again."

"Oh, I almost forgot," Mom said. "I whipped us up a little treat. Who's hungry?"

"I am," LMNOP said, raising her hand as if she were in school.

Aunt Olive muttered, "I could use a little something."

We all followed Mom to the dining-room table and watched as she uncovered her dish of rolled-up tortillas oozing goopy white lumps. They smelled like the bottom of my hamper.

"I learned this recipe in the new cooking class I'm taking down at the high school," she said. "'If at first you don't succeed . . .' Right, Dustin? Oh, we need plates."

Mom disappeared into the kitchen and came back with plates and forks. LMNOP said that the food looked "spectacular" but she really had to run. Then everyone else suddenly felt full and remembered important pretend things they had to do. Lessons or not, nothing could clear a room quicker than Mom's cooking.

"Try one, Dustin." She looked disappointed. "I hate to see good food go to waste."

"Uh, okay. I'm game." I looked down at the plate, wondering if the emergency room was crowded on weekends. "Oh, yeah, Dr. Devon called before to check up on Granny. He said he'd call back – to talk to you."

"What? Why didn't you tell me?"

"I just did."

Mom made a mad dash to the hall mirror and started poofing up her hair, like the doc would be able to see through the phone or something. I picked up one of the drippy blobs, too grossed out to take a bite. Then I got to thinking that in a world where LMNOP was a genius, Jeremy was a pauper, and Gordy was on his way to the opera of his own free will, anything was possible. I closed my eyes and took a sloppy bite. It wasn't half-bad.

"Mom, this is thpectacular!" I said, imitating LMNOP's lisp.

"Are you serious?" She turned to me, beaming. "I can never tell if you're serious."

I nodded yes, smacking my lips to really get the point across.

"Well, that's certainly a first."

Nobody else could make her smile like I could. It was an early Mother's Day present.

"Dee-lish," I said. "What is this thing, anyway?"

"That's a wrap."

The phone rang and she jumped. *Doctor Dreamboat, right on time.* I kept my chewing noises down to a minimum so I could listen in on their conversation.

"Hello? Oh! Fine. Yes, everyone's fine. Listen, I don't think this is a very good idea." Mom's voice sounded weird. Shaky. She leaned against the bureau, rubbing her neck. "I have to say, I'm really in shock that you're calling."

I just told her he was calling back. She never listens.

"Uh-huh. Yes, it was quite an event," she said, looking my way. "We're very proud of him. Of course he was crushed that . . ." She slowly made her way to the windows. "No, I didn't hear about any train derailment. A mile outside of Chicago?" My ears perked up. There was a long pause while Mom just listened, picking at a loose thread on the drapes. "Oh, my God! Are you okay?" she said, lowering herself onto the window seat. "Thank goodness. You were really lucky. Yeah." More pausing and neck rubbing. "Uh, no, he's not. He's spending the night at his –" Mom stopped midsentence. She closed her eyes and took a slow, noisy breath. "Hold on one second."

With the phone muffled against her chest, she quickly wiped her cheek. I had a hard time swallowing what was in my mouth. My face was hot, my heartbeat galloping. I knew what was coming.

"Dustin. It's your dad. Do you want to talk to him?"

Okay, it's no big secret that we're inches away from the

end of the book, so I guess I should be winding up my story. Besides, I've got an important call to take. And it may be a while – Dad and I have lots of catching up to do.

So wish me luck – the *good* kind. And as Mom said a few paragraphs earlier – that's a wrap!

Acknowledgments

At the risk of sounding like I'm making an Academy Awards acceptance speech, there are so many people I want to thank for making this book possible. First off, a wonderful critique group composed of Chris Woodworth, Lisa Williams Kline, Lee P. Sauer, and Manya Tessler, who helped shape my words and gave me much-needed support during the writing process. Even more thanks to Chris for introducing me to my fantastic agent, Steven Chudney. Thanks, Steven, for your professional expertise and consistent belief in me. And as for my editor extraordinaire, Andrea Spooner, what can I say but thank you for getting the best work out of me while remaining a total sweetheart at the same time. Music is swelling – so many others to thank! Andrea's ever-helpful assistant editor, Sangeeta Mehta; my brilliant copyeditor, Katie Gehron. Oh, yes! Tracy Shaw for the incredible book jacket design. And Steve Channon and Dimitry Liaros for their artistic contributions.